Meet Jasper, inventor of the Cat Chat 2000!

Packed with WACKY INVENTIONS!

AT would do if you mega-rich iit?

Written and illustrated by MCLAUGHLIN-JAME

I would buy
100 HORSES!
—PHOEBE

I WOULD BUY ALL THE
FOOTBALL PLAYERS IN
THE WORLD AND MAKE
MY OWN SUPER TEAM
—MYLES

I would
travel the
world
—MADISON

WHAT WOULD
YOU DO WITH
A BILLION
POUNDS?!

I WOULD BUY THE Blue
steam RAILWAY AN
EXTRA TRAINS
THE WORL

I would buy a HUGE mansion so that all my friends and family could come and stay

—ANNA

Buy the world's biggest trampoline!

—ARTIE

LOADS of sweets... AND A goldfish

—JACK

A ROBOT BUTLER!

—Joe AND HARRY

Give some to CHARITY AND go HAVE some FUN

—MAGNUS

To Elle, with love

OXFORD
UNIVERSITY PRESS

Great Clarendon Street, Oxford OX2 6DP
Oxford University Press is a department of the University of Oxford.
It furthers the University's objective of excellence in research, scholarship,
and education by publishing worldwide. Oxford is a registered trade mark of
Oxford University Press in the UK and in certain other countries

Copyright © Tom McLaughlin
The moral rights of the author have been asserted
Database right Oxford University Press (maker)

First published 2017

British Library Cataloguing in Publication Data

Data available

ISBN: 978-0-19-274956-7

1 3 5 7 9 10 8 6 4 2

Printed in Great Britain
Paper used in the production of this book is a natural,
recyclable product made from wood grown in sustainable forests.
The manufacturing process conforms to the environmental
regulations of the country of origin.

THE Accidental
BILLIONAIRE

Written and
illustrated by
Tom McLaughlin

OXFORD
UNIVERSITY PRESS

CHAPTER 1
THIRD WOLVERHAMPTON SCHOOL BLOWS UP!

The room was completely deserted, not a soul to be seen anywhere. Just what Jasper was hoping for. He peeked through the window of the door to double check. This was not the first time Jasper had broken into a room; he considered himself quite the expert. He slipped his school library card between the door and its frame. As he slid it up and down, there was a slight twang and a clunk and with a gentle nudge of his shoulder, he was in. Jasper took a deep breath through his nose.

'Ahhh,' he exhaled, smiling at the familiar smell

of the science lab. It was the place where Jasper felt most at home, the place where he did his greatest work. Sure, there had been the odd mistake, the occasional small explosion, but Jasper reckoned even Michelangelo didn't get his paintings right first time. He probably coloured outside of the lines occasionally. All great artists needed time to master their craft and that's what Jasper was, an artist. If only his science teacher, Mr Smidge, could see that, Jasper wouldn't have to break in at lunchtime and carry out his own experiments. And today would be Jasper's greatest triumph, for at last he would manage to achieve what had evaded the greatest minds for decades: today Jasper was going to realize his dream of creating everlasting custard. Yes, that's right, he was going to invent a custard that would regenerate itself, a bit like Doctor Who, but if Doctor Who was yellow and wobbly and tasted nice on top of sponge pudding. Jasper scanned the lab, looking for what he needed. Suddenly his eyes widened—there it was. The cupboard that contained all the best chemicals. He opened it and stroked the tops of the bottles.

'Lovely, lovely sciencey things . . .' Jasper grinned, grabbing a handful of bottles. 'Yes, I'll need all of these, and one of those too.' He skipped over to the benches, where the Bunsen burners were. He grabbed a glass bowl and a tripod then threw down his rucksack.

'What's that, Nan?' Jasper said loudly to himself. 'You say there's no more custard for your jam sponge? *Au contraire,* Nan. You forgot about Jasper's Everlasting Custard, registered trademark. There'll be no more going short in the custard department for you, Nan. What's that, Nan? Genius, you say? Well, I'm just happy to do my bit for mankind, making the world a happier place with my Everlasting Custard, registered trademark. Yes, the Nobel Prize was a surprise, but when there's enough custard to feed the world, it makes war pretty irrelevant.' Jasper spent a lot of his life pretending to talk to people.

He poured the custard into the bowl and placed it on the tripod over the Bunsen burner. He grabbed the electric lighter and suddenly there was fire.

Jasper reached for the nearest pair of goggles. 'Safety first, don't want any more accidents.'

The custard began to bubble in the bowl. 'Right, all I need to to do is add a bit of this, and a splash of this. That way the genetic make-up of the custard can be replicated.' Jasper watched eagerly as various coloured liquids plunged into the bowl of now-boiling custard. The mixture fizzed and began to rise.

'Oops, that's a little high, let's just turn it down a tad,' Jasper said to himself. 'Oops! That's not down, that's up.' Jasper adjusted the Bunsen burner again. 'Ouch—OK, that's still quite hot. Right, where are the protective gloves?' Jasper looked around and saw the gloves locked away in the cupboard. 'Rightio, OK, no need to panic.' The custard began to boil over and spill down the side of the glass and onto the desk. 'No worries, I'll use my tie instead of gloves.' Jasper grabbed his tie and tried to turn the Bunsen burner down. 'OK, OK, now my tie's on fire. Not to worry. The last thing I must do is panic. My nipples are quite hot though, but not to worry, I can get out of this.' Jasper pulled off his shirt and tie over his head and began to stamp on them. He picked up his singed tie and wiped his brow with the back of his hand. 'Phew, that was close, I thought I was going to cause a . . . FIRE!' he screamed, looking up at the bench.

He'd been so busy stamping out the flames that he hadn't noticed the custard spilling down from the tripod and catching fire. The good news was that Jasper had seemingly found the secret to everlasting custard; the bad news was he'd invented flammable custard at the same time. Jasper grabbed the nearest bottle of water and threw it over the whole mess. The small fire turned into a medium-sized explosion. Jasper looked at the bottle of water and saw that it was labelled 'Ethanol, highly flammable'.

'OK, now is probably the time to panic.' A loud alarm sounded and then the sprinklers kicked in. Suddenly the whole science lab was as damp as a rainforest and soon the hot custard-y fireball sizzled itself out. Jasper, still topless and covered in custard, ran out of the science lab and into the playground just as the first wave of fire engines arrived.

Putting his tie back on, he lined up with the rest of his class behind Mrs Plum, his teacher, as she counted everyone to make sure no one was missing.

'Spam!' yelled Mrs Plum. That's right, Jasper's surname was Spam. As you can imagine, his class-mates hardly ever made jokes about it.

'Oi, Spam Face, why are you not wearing your shirt? Miss, MISS, THE NEW BOY, SPAM SANDWICH, IS NAKED MISS!' a boy called Hector Wiggle helpfully pointed out.

'I am not naked!' Jasper yelled back. 'Look, I clearly have trousers, socks, shoes, and a tie on. Yes, I am shirtless, but I am nearer being dressed than being naked!' This is probably not the best thing to shout when you're in a playground full of school children and you've only been there a week. It was at that point everyone started to laugh. Jasper shook his head. This was turning into a really rotten Tuesday.

'Look, Miss, Jasper's brains have leaked out, look, he has brains on him, Miss,' a girl in Jasper's class said to the teacher, but in that way that meant everyone could hear. Jasper looked down at his custard-covered belly and scooped a bit up with his finger. He licked it. *It's not so bad you know, flame-grilled custard,* Jasper thought to himself as he took a moment to savour the taste.

'EWWW! MISS, MISSSS, SPAM'S EATING HIS OWN BRAINS!' Hector Wiggle hollered, his eyeballs practically flying out of his head. The whole school squirmed in horror.

'Obviously I'm not eating my own brains!' Jasper screamed back. 'You don't have to be a genius to know that would be impossible, I'd be dead. What are you all, morons?'

'All right, Spam, keep it down,' ordered Mrs Plum.

At that moment, five burly firemen came out of the science block and strode over towards Mrs Plum, who immediately started fanning herself with her hands.

'Are you the head teacher?' one of the firemen asked.

'No, that would be me,' said Mr Brooks the

headmaster, barging his way over. 'Hi, I'm Mr Brooks.'

'Chief Fire Officer Stevens. We've located the source of the fire and I'm glad to say that it's out now. It was in the science block, but me and the lads can't work it out, the whole place was filled with ...'

'Filled with what?' Mr Brooks asked.

'Custard,' Stevens replied. 'There was loads of it, quite a mess in there in fact, almost like it was ...'

'It was what?!' Mr Brooks yelled.

'*Everlasting* custard. I know, silly of me, there's no such thing. If only there were, eh, lads?' the chief said with a chuckle to the rest of the firemen. 'Anyway, we're off.'

'Off?' Mrs Plum said, looking sad. 'What if it happens again? I mean, perhaps I should take your number and maybe your address?'

'I suppose giving you my number wouldn't hurt,' Stevens said with a smile. 'Do you have a pen?'

'What, really? Oh yes, I do!' she said, excitedly pulling a pen and a piece of paper from her bag. 'OK, go!'

'My number's 999 ...'

'Nine . . . ni . . . oh.' Mrs Plum sighed.

'Three nines,' said the fireman. 'I'm surprised you don't already know it, to be honest. I mean it's been around a while. What are you, nearly fifty?'

'I'm thirty-two, actually!' Mrs Plum snapped.

'Enough of this, what about the fire? Does anyone know anything about any custard?' Mr Brooks said, eyeing the children.

They all slowly turned and stared at Jasper, who was still busy licking the custard from his belly button.

'SPAAAAAAAAAAAM!'

Mr Brooks screamed.

'MY OFFICE, NOW!'

CHAPTER 2
SEARCH FOR EVERLASTING CUSTARD GOES ON

Jasper sat in Mr Brooks' office, his hands tucked underneath his knees, custard dripping down his belly, the faint whiff of singed hair in the air.

Jasper glanced at Mr Brooks, who was staring at him intently. He was a gruff-looking man with giant ears, the biggest Jasper had ever seen. No matter what he did, Jasper couldn't stop staring at them. Should he say something? he wondered. He probably should, I mean he did just nearly burn down the school; He probably owed Mr Brooks an apology at least.

'I just wanted to say s—'

'Shut it, Spam.'

'Fair enough,' Jasper muttered.

'I've been looking at your educational record. You know, a history of all the other schools you've been to. That's right, schools with an "s".'

'School has always been spelled with an "s", sir,' Jasper said, looking a little perplexed.

'No, the "s" at the end. *Schools.* There have been quite a few.'

'Oh,' Jasper said. 'Yes, I've moved around a bit, I guess.'

'Moved, or been *asked* to move?' Mr Brooks grimaced. 'According to your records, three of your previous schools have burned down.'

'Coincidence,' Jasper snapped.

'All the fires started in the science blocks.'

'Coincidences happen all the time.'

'And you caused all of the fires,' Mr Brooks said, checking his notes.

'I'm not sure what you're getting at, Mr Brooks?' Jasper asked.

'ARE YOU ILL? NOT SURE WHAT I'M GETTING AT?! YOU KEEP BLOWING UP EVERY SCHOOL YOU GO TO!'

'Not every one. Just three out of five.'

'That's still too many. There isn't a correct number of schools that it's OK for you to have blown up. No schools, that's how many I've blown up. That counts as a pupil and a teacher. I've only just started here and I haven't blown it up yet.' Mr Brooks pressed the button on his intercom.

'Miss Jones, how many schools have you blown up?'

'So far today?' Miss Jones replied through the intercom.

'So far today . . .'

'None,' Miss Jones replied. 'By the way, the doctor rang about having your ears pinned back—'

Mr Brooks quickly pressed the button on the intercom. 'I think we've heard enough,' he said, running his fingers through his wispy hair.

'But sir, I'm an inventor.'

'All you've invented, Spam, is exploding schools.'

'It's not true, I've invented lots of things. And anyway, isn't the school motto *Who Dares Wins*?'

'No, that's the SAS, you clot. Our school motto is *Excel in Being Average*.'

'Oh. Well, it doesn't matter. I'm an inventor. All I was doing was fulfilling my potential.'

'All right then, Spam, what have you ever invented? Go on, I'm all ears.'

'So it would seem.'

'What?'

'Nothing,' said Jasper, trying to wipe the smile

from his face. 'I've invented lots of things. Today's attempt at making everlasting custard was less than successful, I grant you. But I made a pair of electric slippers once, so you could see where you were going if you needed a midnight wee.'

'Electric slippers?! What did you do, strap a couple of torches to them?'

'I didn't know you were familiar with my inventions,' Jasper said, scratching his head.

'Oh, for the love of crikey.' Mr Brooks slumped in his chair. 'You leave me with no choice; I'm going to have to expel you. And take my advice: stop trying to be something you're not. I wanted to be a cloud when I was little, but my mother sat me down and told me to stop dreaming and get on with life. Doesn't your mother tell you to stop blowing up schools?'

'I don't really have a mum or dad, just a nan.'

'Oh well, hmm, that's awkward . . . OK, I'm going to be your mother for a moment.'

'Will I have to call you Mummy?'

'No, and don't interrupt.'

'Sorry Mummy.'

'Stop calling me Mummy. Let me be frank—'

'Who's Frank? Is he my dad?'

'Please stop talking and listen. You're not going to be an inventor. You're not going to be rich—'

'Who's Rich?'

'You're not going to have lots of money. You won't be famous either. Now, please get out of my school before I jump out of the window.'

Jasper sighed, then got up and walked out of Mr Brooks' office. He grabbed his school bag, or what was left of it, and headed for the exit. What was his nan going to say? Maybe he could get up every morning and pretend to go to school. Maybe she'd never find out. He was nine, he only had to do it for another seven years or so. Nah, she was bound to notice that he wasn't getting any reports . . . or homework . . . Come to think of it, it was probably his worst idea since he'd invented the hover toaster. Now *that* had been a proper fire. Jasper trundled home, cold, covered in now-lumpy custard, his burnt hair wafting in the wind.

'Evening, Rover,' Jasper said as the ginger tom cat ran up to him and rubbed himself against his legs. Jasper stroked his belly and tickled his ears. Rover purred and looked up at Jasper, his eyes closing with contentment.

'At least someone likes me. Mark my words, Rover. I'll invent something that'll change the world!'

'Meow,' Rover replied.

Jasper had had Rover for as long as he could remember. He liked to think of him as a member of the family rather than just a pet. It was always the three of them, Jasper, Rover and Nan. Jasper's mum and dad weren't around any more; there had been a bad accident years ago. His nan didn't talk about it much. All he knew was that his parents hadn't been all that kind, so Jasper didn't ask. He had Nan and Nan had him and that's all they needed. He sometimes got funny looks when he explained his family situation to people, but he liked it. *What's wrong with being different?* he often thought.

Jasper walked down the garden path towards the front door, put the key in the lock, then took a deep breath and smiled.

'Hi Nan—'

'Not now, sunbeam,' his nan interrupted. She was busy studying the newspaper while the TV blared in the background. 'Come on you beauty. Get in you beauty! It's the three-thirty from Kempton, a dead cert, my lad!' Nan shouted. Nan always shouted, partly because she was slightly hard of hearing and mostly because the TV was always on at full blast. Nan's favourite was the racing. She liked to have a little bet on the horses, but she'd been known to bet on the dogs too. Jasper didn't understand it, really. But Nan always claimed she knew what she was doing.

'I heard from a guy in the pub, whose son works down at the yard, who is friendly with the guy who mucks out the horses, that this is a certain winner. Come on my little beaut, come on number seven!' she yelled.

'Which one's number seven?' Jasper said, hoping a big win might help soften the blow that he'd been kicked out of another school.

'The one in the yellow stripes.'

'The one that's running a different way to the others?' Jasper asked, staring at the TV screen.

'What?! Oh number seven, what are you doing? You're supposed to jump over the fence, not eat it.'

They watched for a few more seconds. 'Is he lying down?' asked Jasper.

'Oh no, not again. Why do I always pick the wrong'uns?'

'He's actually fallen asleep mid-race. I didn't think that was even possible.'

'Bottoms!' Nan yelled as she grabbed the remote and turned off the TV. 'What a donkey.' She turned to Jasper and looked at him for the first time since he'd got home. 'Where's your clothes? Why are you home early? What's that burning smell? Oh no. You didn't, did you? Another school? Jasper!' she sighed.

So much for wondering how to break the news to her, thought Jasper. She'd managed to work it out within two point three seconds, a new record.

'Before you start, Nan, it wasn't my fault.' Jasper took a moment to remember exactly what had happened. 'OK, some of it was my fault, but all I was trying to do was make our fortune. I know I can do it, I can change the world, get us out of this house, so we don't have to worry about money again. I just need to get it right.'

'Jasper, Jasper, I know, lad. You're a genius, you just need to get your break. But we can't keep doing this, we can't keep changing schools. You need an education, son.'

'I know, but I just don't think I'm a school sort of person.'

'You need to learn to listen to adults.'

'I listen to you,' Jasper protested.

'But I'm not your teacher . . .' Nan stopped.

'What is it?'

'Maybe I should be your teacher. I mean I couldn't do any worse than the others.'

'Hmm, well, hmm, it's an interesting idea, but haven't things changed since you were at school?'

'There are certain things that will always stay the same. I could be your teacher, then you could spend more time in the shed, doing science stuff and I'd be on standby in case anything should, you know, explode,' Nan said, rubbing her hands.

'OK, firstly, it's a laboratory, not a shed, secondly . . . Wait, I can't think of a secondly,' Jasper said.

'That's because it's a great idea!' Nan smiled.

'Meow,' Rover added.

'You see, even the cat agrees!' Nan laughed.

'Oh well, if the cat agrees, I guess we have to do it.' Jasper shrugged. 'I suppose it would give me more time to work on my inventions . . .'

'Brilliant, we'll 'ave a hoot. I mean, how hard can it be?'

CHAPTER 3
HOME SCHOOLING ON THE RISE

'Morning!' CLANGALANGALANG!

Jasper woke with a jump. Well, a jump and a scream. There at the end of his bed was his nan, shaking a bell at him. She was for some reason draped in what appeared to be a black cape.

'What on earth, Nan! Are you trying to give me a heart attack?'

'Nonsense, it's good for you,' she yelled, shaking the bell again.

'Are you dressed as Batman?'

'No.'

'Er, Batnan?' Jasper said, trying to stop the ringing in his ears.

'No! I'm a teacher. I'm wearing one of those teacher gowns they wear on the TV, you know, to look like a teacher. Look, I've even got one of those square hat thingies.'

'That's a chessboard. And it's not a gown, it's a bin bag.'

'I know, clever ain't I?'

'But why?'

'I told you, I'm dressed as a teacher. Now stick this on.' Jasper's nan threw him a bundle of clothes.

'What's this?'

'It's your games kit. First lesson, ain't it?' Nan grinned and pulled a whistle out of her back pocket.

'You have got to be kidding me,' Jasper said with a yawn. 'I thought having you as my teacher would be easier than school. You know, a little light baking followed by double bingo.'

'Don't be cheeky, or you'll have to spend this evening in detention,' warned Nan. She let out a shrill peep on her whistle. 'I'll see you on the green outside in five minutes! Don't be late or I'll give you the cane.'

'You're not allowed to hit kids at school any more,' Jasper said sleepily.

'Really? I'll have to put the canes back on the runner beans plants then. Five minutes!' she said, before blowing her whistle even louder.

A few moments later Jasper emerged onto the patch of grass known as the green in front of their house. In the middle of it, holding a ball, stood his nan, now not only in a bin bag cape, but also baggy shorts and what looked like dance shoes. It could have been worse, she could have been in the world's tiniest shorts . . . but Jasper was wearing those. Fortunately, his nan's large blouse, that he was also forced to wear, came down to his knees, which was humiliating but also quite handy.

'Why do I have to wear this? I look like an idiot,' Jasper sighed, trying to find his hands that were dangling somewhere up his enormous sleeves.

'I couldn't find your games kit,' said Nan. 'So I had to make do.'

'It's still at school, I didn't get a chance to collect it before they threw me out.'

'Well good news, sunbeam, you can't ever get expelled from my school.'

'Oh good . . .'

'Right, we're going to have a game of association football. I've dug out your grandpa's old football. This made it back from Dunkirk you know. Now I'm a little rusty on the rules, but I remember the basics. I'm going to throw it up and I want you to do a head thingy, you know where the ball hits your head? I don't know what it's called.'

'A header, Nan,' said Jasper. 'Nan, can I ask why we're doing this now? There's a lot of people on their way to work. They're looking.' A small crowd had gathered around the green.

'Football's a spectator sport, now do a head thingy.' Nan threw the ball up in the air. Fortunately for Jasper, he was pretty good at football. He wasn't the best—he blinked and flinched a lot in tackles—but he had a mean right foot on him when he wanted. Jasper rose like a salmon, a salmon in very tight shorts and an old lady's blouse, but a salmon all the same. *THWACK!* Jasper met the ball and immediately let out a howl of pain.

'WHAT'S THAT BALL MADE OF, ROCKS?!' Jasper said, rolling around and clutching his head. 'Am I bleeding?'

Nan rushed over and reached into her pocket.

'Yellow card!' She peeped on her whistle.

'What?' Jasper cried, still in a considerable amount of pain.

'Yellow card. No one was anywhere near you. You dived.'

'Dived? I've just been hit in the head with this!' Jasper grabbed the ball. 'Whatever this is. I mean I know what it definitely *isn't,* and that's a football. I've felt a football before, but this was like trying to head a meteorite.'

'Right, that's it, another yellow for giving me gyp. You're off, sonny Jim.'

'Giving you gyp, you're booking me for that?' Jasper argued.

'I'm bored now. It's time for the next lesson, inside we go!' Nan said in her new and quite annoying teacher voice.

Jasper followed Nan into the living room, where there was a desk with an assortment of books neatly laid out in the middle.

'Next up, the three Rs! Reading, writing and arithmetic. Any questions?'

Jasper put his hand up straight away.

'Err, yes, the boy in the middle,' said Nan.

'What do the three Rs stand for?' Jasper said, looking confused.

'Reading, writing and arithmetic . . . I just told you. So anyway, the most important thing when it comes . . . yes, the boy in the middle, do you have another question?'

'You do know, of the three Rs, only one begins with "r"?'

'Look, it was good enough in my day, sonny Jim,' Nan barked.

'All I'm saying is that if you want to teach writing, telling people that it begins with an "r", isn't the best start. Also, while we're at it, if you're talking about arithmetic—which is maths, right?'

'Yes.' Nan sighed.

'Well then. Telling people there are three "r"s, when mathematically speaking there's only one, it's not great, I'll be honest with you. Don't you agree, Rover?' Jasper looked at the cat, who was busy sleeping.

'Rightio, read the first five chapters of *War and*

Peace until lunch in that case.' Nan huffed. 'You know, I'm beginning to see why you got thrown out of so many schools.'

'Have you finished with your mint pea and broccoli soup?' Nan said dressed as a dinner lady.

'Yes, it's like someone caught a sneeze in a bowl,' Jasper grimaced taking his last sip.

'Great, let's do a bit of science then.'

'Yes!' Jasper said, punching the air.

'Open your books, we're going to do the facts of life.'

Jasper looked down and opened a well-thumbed copy of *Human Biology for Dummies* and gulped.

Three and half hours later, Jasper said, 'Well, I'll never sleep again.'

'What do you mean? That was very thorough.'

'I'll say. We had ages on you and Grandpa's court-ship during the war, then there was something about birds and bees, then you winked a lot and said "know what I mean" seven times.'

'Oh stop moaning, that was a pretty good day!' Nan said taking off her chessboard and bin bag cape. 'Nothing exploded and you didn't get expelled. Progress, sunshine! Let's call it a day.'

'Yeah, I suppose,' Jasper said. 'I'm shattered.'

'I'll get us some tea on, then I'll have to go to work,' Nan said, shuffling off into the kitchen.

'Do you have to? It's late—you must be tired too.'

'I am, but I need to go to work. Mr Dank relies on me.'

'That man's a meanie, only interested in counting his money,' Jasper sniped.

'He's all right—he just likes to have his bathrooms spick and span, lad.'

'Well, he should pay you more for the hours you work.'

'If it wasn't for him we wouldn't be able to live in such luxury. Beans for supper?' she chuckled.

'Yeah, OK, thanks Nan.'

'Cleaning that big mansion round the corner pays pretty well. Plus I get to have a nose around the place. Do you know they have six bathrooms? Six!

Can you believe that?'

Jasper was suddenly hit with a wave of sadness. He didn't know how old Nan was; every time he asked, she would tell him 'a lady never tells and a gent never asks'. What he did know was that she was too old to be working. Everyone else's grandparents were retired, having a rest, going on long holidays on coaches. But not Nan. She worked hard just so they could get by.

'If only there was a way to make us all rich, Rover,' he said. The cat had finally woken up. 'It must be time for your tea too, I guess.'

Nan came in a few seconds later with some 'toast under beans'. A clever new twist on beans on toast, she liked to say.

'Right, eat up,' Nan said as they both tucked in. 'You too, Rover!'

Rover let out a sleepy meow.

'I wonder what he would say if he could speak.' Nan smiled and gave him a pat on the head. 'Anyway, I've got to shoot off.'

'Before you go, have you got it with you?'

Jasper asked, scooping a big spoonful of beans into his mouth.

'Yes, always.' Nan whipped out her walkie-talkie helmet that consisted of an old motorcycle helmet with a radio and coat hanger aerial.

'The good old Nan Chat 5!' Jasper said. One of his few successful inventions, it allowed him and his nan to communicate with each other when she was out working, just in case there was a problem.

'I wouldn't be without it!' she chuckled. 'Now straight to bed, no weird inventions and I'll kiss you goodnight when I get home.'

Nan collected her mops, opened the front door and went out into the night. There was a chill from the outside—Jasper would have hated to go out into this weather. How his nan must feel, he couldn't imagine. Jasper looked at Rover.

'I'm close to the big invention.' Jasper grinned, popping on his Nan Chat helmet. 'I've been thinking about something for a while now that will make free electricity. Imagine that, Rover.'

Rover meowed.

'I know, I'm pretty excited too. Imagine if it worked; I'd be a millionaire, maybe even a billionaire! We could live in a house with all those bathrooms. I know Nan said no experiments, but one wouldn't hurt, would it? Just quickly, before she gets back.'

CHAPTER 4
TURNS OUT SPLITTING THE ATOM IS MUCH HARDER THAN YOU THINK

Jasper headed down to the shed, Rover snaking between his legs. The light was fading, and Jasper felt the chill in his lungs. He yanked open the door, removed his Nan Chat helmet and took a deep breath. The shed smelled of old tins of paint, rusty lawnmowers, and dust hanging in the air.

Jasper closed his eyes. 'I can almost taste it, Rover, this is going to be the one. This is the one they'll all remember me for.'

Rover looked up and opened his mouth, as if to meow in agreement, but instead out came a big yawn.

'Calm down boy, you're getting overexcited again,' Jasper said with a smile.

The shed was like no other shed you've seen—it was more a laboratory with a few spades in it. Jasper hit the button by the door, and suddenly the whole place came to life. Various old computers and laser machines that Jasper had rescued over the years began bleeping and flashing randomly. The overhead lights blinked on and shelves of test tubes began to bubble and fizz. Jasper grabbed his goggles and looked around for his tools.

'Here's the plan, Rover. We're going to change the way the world works. We're going to recreate the Big Bang and harness all that energy. I'm going to break the very fabric of time in order to tap into the infinite energy of space and the surrounding cosmos. In short, Rover, I'm going to split the atom. Yes, that's right, split the atom. I'm going to need three things. A very large mallet, a teeny tiny chisel, and a good eye.' Jasper pulled his goggles on. 'Now if all goes well, I will have managed to extract power from the very building blocks of life.

If all doesn't go well, I will cause an explosion that may wipe out life on Earth. Let's hope for the first one. Rightio, good luck Rover, I shall see you on the other side.' Jasper nodded to the cat, who jumped up onto the window ledge.

Jasper grabbed the largest of all his mallets and his tiny chisel. 'All I need now is an atom,' he said, looking around. 'Well, I guess, as the whole world is made of atoms, there's one right here.' He squinted at the workbench beneath the laser machine.

'OK, after three,' Jasper said, placing the chisel on the worktop. 'One . . . twooo . . .' He took a deep breath. 'Threeeeee!' He swung the mallet back so he could thwack it on top of the chisel. But at the moment of his backswing, the head of the mallet flew off and smashed into the test tubes behind him, and before he knew it there was bubbling liquid flying everywhere. A huge globule landed on the laser machine and short-circuited the wires. Suddenly it started firing random red lasers out in every direction. They flew around the shed, bouncing off the windows and metal garden tools.

Jasper dived to the ground and put his hands over his head, as if he was in the middle of an earthquake.

'Crikey, that nearly burned my bottom off!'

Jasper stood up slowly and turned towards the direction the voice had come from.

'Who said that?' he said in shock. Had Nan come back early? Was he being watched?

'ARRGH!' Rover yelled.

'AAAAAAARGHHHH!' Jasper yelled back.

'ARRRRRRRRRRGGGGGGGGG-HHHHHHHH!' they both yelled.

'YOU CAN TALK!' Jasper shrieked.

'YOU CAN HEAR ME!' Rover cried.

'YES! I CAN HEAR YOU BECAUSE YOU CAN TALK. ME BEING ABLE TO HEAR ISN'T THAT UNUSUAL. THE BIG NEWS HERE IS THAT YOU CAN TALK! HOW?!' Jasper said, jumping up and down with either excitement or fright—he couldn't quite work it out. It was a bit of both, like being on a rollercoaster after eating a big bag chips. He felt brilliant, but also like he might throw up at any second. 'WHAT HAPPENED?'

'I don't know. I was watching you about to split the atom, then that big hammer thingy flew off and hit the laser, then the laser hit the window, then the other window, then the spade, then the test tube, then the window again, then the thing that's like a tiny spade, then the bucket . . .'

'YES, YES, GET TO THE END!'

'Hey! It's not my fault I have excellent attention to detail. Anyway, you asked. Before I knew what had happened the laser beam went in my bottom and then you started shouting at me!'

'Can I see?' Jasper said.

'What?' Rover replied.

'Your bottom.'

'What's wrong with you? I'm the first talking cat and you want to look at my bottom. What are you, a dog? They love bottoms; it's all they do, all day long. Sniffing bottoms, I don't understand the fascination. Weird creatures if you ask me. Bottoms and postmen, they're just obsessed.'

'I just want to see!' Jasper said.

'Oh, very well, but you're only demeaning yourself.' Rover sighed and turned round.

'I see, yes. I can smell it from here.'

'Well, that's charming, isn't it,' Rover tutted. 'In case you hadn't noticed, the important bit is happening up the other end. The mouth end.'

'No, I meant I can smell the singed fur. I think what I've done is fired a laser beam up your bottom,' Jasper said.

'I know you have, I was there. Did you not hear me just tell you that? Are you sure your hearing's OK?' Rover said, shaking his little furry head.

'It must have travelled straight up and genetically

changed your vocal chords, fused them together and somehow linked to your brain. Meaning that you can talk . . . Do you know what this means?' Jasper said, still staring at Rover's bottom.

'No, what?'

'Nor me, but it must be big!' Jasper said.

'Hello Jasper, how's it all going?'

'Wow, you can even do impressions of my nan!' Jasper cried excitedly. 'This is too much!'

'That wasn't me,' Rover sighed. 'I think it was that thing . . .' He looked over towards Jasper's Nan Chat helmet.

'Nan!' Jasper squealed, grabbing his walkie-talkie. 'I think you need to get back here, it's all gone a bit weird. I mean everything's fine, just deeply, deeply weird. Over and out!'

'What? I'll be there as soon as I can!' Nan cried back.

'Smooth!' Rover said, grinning. 'How are we going to tell her? You'll have to break it to her gently, she's quite an old lady. We don't want anything bad to happen to her.'

'What do you mean?' Jasper said, still trying to get his head around the fact he was talking to a cat.

'All I'm saying is that if I go in and say, "Hello, Nan, how was work?" she may well have a funny turn. We need her safe and well, mate.'

'Hmm, you have a point. OK, I'll go inside and break the news gently to her, then you come in and show you can talk. Oh, this is so weird . . .' Jasper rubbed his eyes, his brain racing in a million different directions.

'Tell me about it. It's pretty weird for me too,' said Rover. 'Plus I had a laser beam fired up my bottom. I'll be trumping smoke rings for a week.'

CHAPTER 5
EXERCISE CAN MAKE THE OLD FEEL YOUNG AGAIN

Jasper ran up the garden path and through the back door, just as Nan's key started to turn in the lock.

'Nan!' he cried.

'All right my lad, what's going on, are you hurt?' Panic was written across Nan's face.

'No, I've never been better!' Jasper grinned.

Nan put down her mops immediately. 'Right, what have you done?' she snapped.

'What?' Jasper said. 'Done? Hahaha . . .' His laughter tailed off awkwardly.

'Have you set fire to the shed?'

'No!' Jasper thought for a second. 'No, the shed is fine.'

'Have you turned the microwave into a helicopter?'

'No! Although you could, all you'd need is a . . .'

'Jasper! Have you turned your pants into jam?'

'Noooooo!' Jasper shook his head in disbelief. 'That was a one-off, I told you it'd never happen again. Everything's fine. Better than fine, in fact.'

'I know you better than you know yourself, sunbeam. I know when you're lying; I know when you've been expelled from school. I know when you're up to something.'

'Oh Nan, you are such a wag.' Jasper smiled. 'I did pop down to the shed . . . you know, for a bit of homework . . .'

'Here it comes . . .' Nan said.

Just at that second came the familiar noise of the cat flap opening. In waltzed Rover, two dead mice in his mouth. He spat them out. 'Man is it cold out there. Could we please get a litter tray, or better still, put a cat flap in the toilet door? Now, I know you two have already eaten, but I caught these couple of beauts in the garden, so who's in the mood for mouse? I was thinking we could pan-fry them with some garlic, possibly open that bottle of Chateauneuf Du Pape which I know you've been keeping for a special occasion, then sit back and watch the match.' Rover looked at Jasper, then back at Nan. 'Oh. You haven't told her, have you?'

'WHHAAAAAAAAA!' Nan let out a blood-curdling scream that shook the whole house. 'KILL IT!!!!!!' she continued to cry, removing her slipper and going after Rover's head.

'Eeek!' Rover yelled, running across the sofa. Nan gave chase, slipper in hand. She dived over the coffee table and legged it across the sofa. Pretty impressive for a woman of her age, whatever her age was.

'CALL THE POLICE WHILE I GET THE MONSTER!' she bellowed.

'It's not a monster, Nan, it's Rover . . . he can talk now!' Jasper said.

'What kind of witchcraft is this?' Nan cried as she threw her copy of *Woman's Weekly* at Rover, just missing his head.

'Stop chasing me, I only have little legs!' Rover panted as he scurried underneath the sideboard.

'Jasper,' Nan cried. 'Get the cricket bat!'

'Excellent idea. A nice game of cricket will calm the nerves,' Jasper said encouragingly.

'I'm going to smash him up!'

'Nan!' Jasper waved his arms around like a traffic policeman.

'Wait a second, I need a rest.' Nan sat down in the armchair.

'I can't keep up this pace any more, I'm not seventy you know.'

'Yeah, can we just take a breather? I feel really dizzy and if I'm honest, a bit sick, although that might have something to do with the moth I ate while pooing in the flowerbeds.' Rover looked at Nan, Nan looked back at Rover. 'Oops!'

'Why you little . . . !' she began. 'Wait, you pooed in the flowerbeds, like a cat?'

'Well, yes. I am a cat!'

'I thought you were like a witch's spell or something?' Nan said, looking a lot less menacing.

'No, I'm just me, except Jasper shot a laser up my bottom and now I can talk,' Rover explained.

'Jasper!' Nan grimaced, 'how many times have I told you to stop messing around?'

'I know, I know,' Rover agreed, 'but will he listen?'

'Will he heck.' Nan rolled her eyes.

'Hello!' Jasper said, getting flustered. 'A talking cat, I made a talking cat! Can we look at the bigger picture here?' He pointed furiously at Rover.

Nan took a deep breath, half-closed her eyes and prodded Rover with a finger.

'So you can really talk?' she said slowly.

'Yep, I know. Crazy times. Hi, I'm Rover.' He waved a paw.

'A laser beam up your bottom?' Nan raised an eyebrow.

'Yep, who knew, huh?'

'Can I see?' Nan asked.

'What's wrong with you people?!' Rover said, exasperated. 'No you can't, there's nothing to see.'

'But how did it happen?' Nan stared at Rover.

'All I've done is connect his vocal chords to his brain,' said Jasper. 'He can talk, but he's still a cat. He still does basic cat stuff, eat mice, do his business in the flowerbeds, but now we can have a chat too.'

'Wow!' Nan mouthed, slowly taking it all in. 'You thought of this?' She looked at Jasper proudly.

'No, he wanted to split the atom, then his mallet broke,' Rover said.

'Shhh!' Jasper said quickly.

'What?' asked Nan, twiddling her hearing aid.

'Nothing, Nan!'

'Amazing, Jasper. You've done something amazing. Truly amazing.'

'You certainly have,' Rover agreed, 'even if you didn't mean to.'

'Maybe I will open that bottle of fizz after all!' Nan grinned.

'BOOM!' Rover said, doing a little paw-pump.

'You're too young to drink.' Nan shook her head at Rover.

'What?!'

'You're nine.'

'In cat years, but in human years, I'm . . .' He started to count the claws on his paws. 'Actually, this is hard without opposable thumbs. In human years, I'm really old. I'd probably work in a bank or something. Maybe have a couple of kids and drive a boring car. Surely I'm allowed a little champagne!'

'No!' Nan yelled, 'you're the world's first talking cat. Who knows what might happen if you have a slurp of wine.'

'She's right. You might start barking like a dog, or your newly lasered bottom might explode,' Jasper said nervously.

'Oh man, this isn't fair,' Rover sighed.

Nan reached into her knitting bag next to the chair. 'How about a nice ball of wool for you?'

'Wool? I can't be bought off with wool . . . even if it is so fresh-looking . . . NO, I mustn't. I'm better than this.' Rover began to twitch.

'Are you sure? Not even if I dangle it above your head . . .?' Nan said tantalizingly.

'No! It isn't going to work. Things have changed now, I'm not just another cat . . . oh, who am I kidding,

I love wool!' Rover skipped over to try and catch it. 'Wool, glorious wool!' He laughed as he pulled it with his paws and rolled around in it. 'Oh yeah, baby, that's the good stuff!'

Nan got up and headed towards the kitchen. She shot Jasper a look for him to follow.

'Everything all right, Nan?' Jasper asked, shutting the door behind him.

'Look lad, I ain't interested in how you did this, and I don't really know what it all means. But what I do know is that things will probably never be the same for us again.'

Jasper gulped. She was right. Somehow, with the help of a flying mallet and a laser beam, Jasper had changed the world forever.

'Are you cross with me, Nan?' he said, suddenly feeling very small indeed.

'No my lad, not at all. I always knew you had greatness in you. We just have to be careful. I mean, when someone sees and hears Rover for the first time, well, it's a little scary. I was scared.'

'You wanted to kill him with a cricket bat,' Jasper agreed.

'Exactly. Someone might try to steal Rover, or hurt him. Or try to take him away from us. We have to look after each other right now.'

'You're right.' Jasper nodded. 'We have to look after each other. Let's go talk to Rover, but try not to spook him.'

'Good plan. Last thing we want is for Rover to go—'

'MISSING!' Jasper yelled, opening the door. He ran into the living room, but Rover was nowhere to be seen. In the back door the cat flap was still flapping.

CHAPTER 6
MISSING CAT
KITNAPPED?

The next morning Jasper and Nan awoke early on the sofa. They'd been up late, walking the streets, hunting high and low, but there had been no sign of Rover.

'Roverrrr!' Jasper said, sitting bolt upright.

Nan rubbed the sleep from her eyes and pulled the *Racing Post* off her face, leaving an imprint of the 2.45 from Wolverhampton on her wrinkled forehead. They both scanned the living room. Nothing.

'Shall we call the police?' Jasper asked.

'For a missing cat? They'll laugh at us,'

Nan replied. 'We've already phoned the local paper.'

'We could tell them it's a talking cat,' Jasper suggested.

'Oh yes, they'd definitely take us seriously in that case.'

'You're right,' Jasper agreed. 'They'd think we'd gone crackers of the noggin.'

I'll make some tea,' Nan yawned. 'And maybe some toast. Then we'll head out again.'

'I'm not hungry.'

'Neither am I, but we need to keep our strength up.' Nan got to her feet. 'Can you fetch the milk in from the front?'

Jasper headed to the door. Their house was still one of the few places that got their milk from a milkman. Nan didn't trust supermarkets when it came to such important matters as putting stuff in your tea. Jasper yawned a big yawn and opened the door.

'Morning!' In strolled Rover, like it was the most normal thing in the world. 'I would have picked up the papers and some croissants, but I left without my wallet and also I don't have a wallet.'

'Where have you been?' Jasper cried. 'We've been worried sick!'

'Oh don't, I'm having a nightmare. I popped out last night for another visit to the flowerbeds—all that excitement plays havoc with my guts. In fact, Nan, I'd probably avoid that part of the garden for a while.'

'You were out all night though!' Nan cried.

'I know, I'm a cat, it's what we do. I've stayed out all night loads of times; you've never worried before.'

Jasper and Nan looked at each other. Rover had a point.

'Anyway, after doing the do, I went for a little walk, you know, clear the nostrils, and before I knew what was what, I was chasing birds.'

'Well, that's no way to behave. You leave the girls alone!' Nan said gruffly.

'No, not girls, actual birds,' Rover clarified.

'Oh, yeah, that would make more sense.'

'Anyway, long story short, I climbed a tree to catch one, and what do you know, I got stuck. Classic cat mistake. When will we learn, huh? I was there all night, shouting for help but no one came.'

'We've been looking for you all night!' Jasper cried. 'We didn't hear you.'

'All right, maybe I only shouted for a few moments before having a little nap.'

'How little?' Jasper said.

'A little eight-hour nap . . .' Rover said tentatively.

'Yeah, that's called falling asleep. If you ask me, anything over twenty minutes doesn't count as a nap,' Jasper said crossly.

'All right, all right, don't punish me for being a cat. We're a sleepy species, what can I say?'

Rover shrugged.

'How did you get down?'

'. . .'

'Wake up, Rover, you're falling asleep again!' Nan cried.

'Oh right, yeah.' Rover shook himself awake. 'So I jumped. I plucked up the courage and jumped. You two would have been dead proud of me.' Rover gave them a wink.

'Jumped or fell?' Jasper said looking at the grass stains on Rover's leg.

'Doesn't matter. The important thing is I'm here now!' Rover grinned. 'What's for brekkie? I'm in the mood for pancakes.'

Just then the doorbell rang. Everyone looked at each other before it rang twice more. Nan got up and headed to the door. 'Eek! It's Mr Dank, the fella I clean for,' Nan cried, looking through the peephole.

There was a knock and the bell rang again. 'I can hear you in there!' a loud voice boomed.

'I bet he's mad I left early last night,' Nan said, looking worried.

'Let him in, I'll explain,' said Jasper. 'He can't get mad at me, I'm a kid. Once he knows you had to be home for me he'll be fine.'

'Yeah, and if he isn't I'll karate chop him in the spleen!' Rover said, wailing like a ninja.

'No!' Nan cried. 'Rover, be quiet. If he hears you talking, well goodness knows what'll happen!'

'She's right, Rover. Keep schtum!' Jasper agreed.

Nan slowly opened the door. 'Oh Mr Dank, how are you?'

Mr Dank walked in. He was a large man with orange skin, and he was wearing lots of shiny watches and rings. It was like he was trying to tell everyone how much money he had. His hair was suspiciously dark for a man of his age and he was as tall as he was wide.

'Why did you leave early yesterday?' he spluttered. 'I didn't give you the day off, and I need my bogs cleaned. If you can't do it, I'll get someone who can!'

Jasper had never met Mr Dank before. He'd walked past his house many times, but the wall was too high to see over and there were too many security cameras for Jasper to take a proper nose. He'd always wondered what sort of man lived in such a big house. Now Jasper had his answer: a rude man. A man who only cared about how clean his toilets were, not about the people who cleaned them.

'Well, I had to get back,' Nan tried to explain, 'to look after my grandson. It's just me and him, you see. He needed me.'

'Save your sob stories. Just don't leave early again or you'll be out on your ear,' Mr Dank shouted, sounding like a very angry foghorn. He headed towards the door.

'Woah, woah, WOAH! Don't talk to her like that, you massive sparkly carrot,' Rover yelled back. Jasper put his hand over his face. The plan for getting rid of Mr Dank as quickly as possible without alerting him to a talking cat had lasted exactly thirteen seconds.

Mr Dank turned round and looked at Jasper.

'What did you say to me, you insubordinate little twonk?' he boomed.

'Err . . .' said Jasper. 'Nothing, I was talking to myself. It was a joke. You know us kids and our crazy sense of humour. I didn't mean anything by it, haha! I actually like carrots.' He gulped. 'Do you like carrots?'

'What's the matter with your grandson, Mrs Spam?' asked Mr Dank. 'He's not one of these weirdos is he, the ones you hear about on the news, doing weird things all the time and getting into trouble? Lock them up and throw away the key, I say!'

'No!' Nan yelled.

'NO!' Jasper yelled.

'That's a funny-looking cat, is he all right?' Mr Dank said, taking a closer look at Rover. 'It's like he's doing karate or something. I have a cat, she's very expensive you know. A pedigree. What's yours, a mongrel?'

'Oh, that's Rover, don't mind him. He's had a fall today, he's not himself,' Jasper said.

'Anyway, I have to go now. Goodbye, Spams. Goodbye, Rover.'

'Goodbye,' Rover replied through gritted teeth. 'I mean, meow,' he said hastily.

'WHAT!' Mr Dank yelled, barely able to believe his ears. 'Your cat just spoke to me. He said "goodbye"!'

'I said "meow"!' Rover protested. 'I mean, meow. Drat, I keep getting it wrong. Am I saying "meow" or "goodbye"?' Rover looked at Jasper for help. Jasper put his hand over his face again.

'He did it again! He spoke to me!' Mr Dank yelled.

'Nonsense!' Jasper replied. 'You imagined it, maybe you've had too much sun.'

'"Maybe"?' Rover interrupted. 'There's no "maybe" about it. He's more orange than me, and I'm a flipping ginger cat! I mean, meow. Sorry, I talked again didn't I?' Rover sighed. 'And anyway, why am I saying sorry—you should be apologizing, the way you spoke to Nan.' He pointed a paw at Mr Dank.

'Oh my word, a talking cat!' Mr Dank said. 'I want one. I want *him*.'

'I'm not for sale!' Rover said. 'Anyway, I wouldn't want to be owned by you. I've seen the way you treat people.'

'I don't understand, how does he talk? Is it a

gizmo?' Mr Dank said, looking for the hidden microphone that wasn't there.

'My Jasper did it. He's a genius, not a weirdo,' Nan said proudly.

'Not a weirdo, you say? All right, name your price!' Mr Dank smiled enticingly.

'He already told you, he's not for sale,' Jasper said, clutching Rover tightly. 'Especially to someone as rude as you!'

'Jasper, that's my boss!' Nan snapped.

'The boy's right!' Mr Dank said, suddenly turning on the charm and yet somehow managing to be even more charmless. 'You're right, I'm sorry, I'm rude. I apologize for my gruff ways. What about if you make my cat talk? I'll be the talk of the country club!'

'It's going to cost you!' Rover jumped in.

'Well, how much?'

'How much do you have?'

'Rover, I'm not sure this is a good idea!' Jasper tried to say, but it was too late.

'I have millions,' Mr Dank said proudly.

'Yes, we'll have one of those,' Rover said.

'Err, OK, a million it is!' Mr Dank said. 'It's a bargain, for a talking cat. I'll bring Precious round this afternoon.' He hurried away.

There was silence in the living room.

'Well, that was a pretty good start to the day. Mr Dank apologized and he's going to give us a million, whatever that is,' Rover said. 'Right, about these pancakes . . . '

'A million,' Jasper said to Nan.

'A million!' Nan grinned.

'What *is* a million?' Rover asked.

'It's a million pounds,' Jasper said, smiling.

'Is that a lot?'

'Yes, it's a million pounds!' Nan cried.

'Well, how am I meant to know? I'm a cat, I have no concept of money, let alone numbers!' Rover said defensively.

'I can't believe it!' Nan cackled. 'Our ship's finally come in. You've done it, Jasper!' She broke into a dance, swinging Jasper by the arm.

'Ha! We did it! No more cleaning jobs for you, no more beans for tea, we're going to be rich, rich I tell you!' Jasper laughed.

'I know, and all you have to do is what you did to Rover! Rover . . . Rover, wake up!' But it was too late, Rover had fallen asleep.

'Haha! Poor thing.' Jasper smiled thoughtfully. 'Yes, all I have to do is what I did to Rover. All I have to do . . .' He paused. 'What *did* I do?' It had been an accident. How could he do it again?

CHAPTER 7
PEOPLE GO NUTS OVER FRENCH SQUIRREL

'I might put the kettle on and have a celebratory cup of tea,' Nan said, dancing off into the kitchen.

'Great idea, Nan!' Jasper grinned awkwardly. He waited until Nan had left the the room before starting to shake Rover awake.

'What's wrong?' Rover said, looking confused.

'What's wrong? Mr Dank is expecting a talking cat. He wants me to make his cat talk and I don't know how! That's what's wrong.'

'Relax, just do what you did before.'

'I don't KNOW what I did before! That's the

problem,' Jasper said. 'I think I'm having a heart attack. I can feel a pounding in my chest.'

'Right, you need to calm down. Why don't you have a saucer of milk and maybe play with a ball of string? Always works for me,' Rover said, smiling.

'I'm not a cat!' Jasper snapped.

'I'm not a giraffe!' Rover yelled back. 'What game are we playing?'

'Oh my word, milk isn't going to calm me down!' Jasper said. 'Seriously, I can feel my heart beating so loud. It's like I can't breathe.'

'You have to calm down. I'm not going to give you the kiss of life,' Rover said, shaking his head.

'I don't want you to give me a kiss; I know where your mouth's been!' Jasper said in disgust.

'Oi, it's my mouth,' Rover snapped back. 'If we're going to do this again, we need everything to be set up exactly the same as before. I have, as we know, an excellent memory. We don't need to know how it happened, just what we did to make it happen.'

'OK, you're right. Let's go. Don't give the game away to Nan,' Jasper said, tapping his nose.

'I got your back, J-man,' Rover said as they strolled down the garden path, whistling casually. Jasper looked around nervously as they stepped into the shed. It was the first time he'd been back since he'd made Rover talk.

'Hey, relax, man. This what you always wanted,' said Rover. 'You can do this. I believe in you.'

'Is everything in the right place?' Jasper asked.

'How do I know? Just because I've noticed that that laser was one and half centimetres to the left, and that mirror was at an angle of thirty-six point seven degrees, it doesn't mean I know everything . . . oh!' Rover said. 'Maybe I *can* help.'

An hour later, the shed was an exact replica of how everything had been the previous night. Jasper patted Rover on the head. 'Well done, lad.'

'Pleasure. What now, the pub?' Rover asked.

'No! Now . . . now . . .' Jasper hesitated. 'Now . . . we test it.' He grabbed the mallet and positioned himself. 'Was I standing about here last night?' he asked.

'Yep,' nodded Rover. 'Now try a practice swing.'

'OK.' Jasper took a swing and the mallet flew out of his hand. 'Bloomin' Nora, I've done it again!'

he cried. There was a *ping* and several flashes as a laser beam bounced around the shed before flying out of the window.

'BLIMEY! THAT WAS CLOSE! STOP DOING THAT!' Rover cried out, darting over to the window to see where the laser landed.

'Sorry, sorry, my bad, my bad. Is everyone OK?' Jasper said.

'Well, there's a squirrel in the garden speaking French . . .'

'Ooh, awkward,' Jasper said, peering out through the window. 'The good news is that it worked again. I mean, apart from the French bit.' Jasper looked at the laser machine. 'I think the laser only works when the animal's mass is at the optimum level.'

'What? Speak English, man!' Rover complained.

'It means that cats are the right size, dogs would be too big, squirrels too small. Things malfunction if it's not a cat.'

'Yes, I knew it. In. Your. Face. Dogs! Cats win!'

Rover said, doing a little victory dance.

'Quite finished, have we?' Jasper said.

'Sorry, but it's nice to know who finally won that argument. Do you think the machine will work?' Rover asked.

'Maybe. Either we'll make history or we'll break Mr Dank's cat and make it meow numbers or sneeze in Chinese.'

'I guess we'll find out soon enough,' Rover said, looking out of the window. The light was failing and there was a set of headlights shining through the front window and down the garden. He gulped. 'I think Dank is here.'

CHAPTER 8
WORLD'S MOST EXPENSIVE CAT SOLD

'Get that rat out of my house!' Nan cried at the top of her voice, standing on a chair trying to shoo something away with a broom. Yes, people do that in real life, not just in cartoons. Rover and Jasper glanced around to see what the fuss was about. There in the middle of the room stood Mr Dank, looking very annoyed by the whole situation. Next to him was a thing. A creature of sorts, but 'a thing' seems to sum it up better.

'Arrgh! What on earth is that?' Rover screamed.

'It's my cat,' Mr Dank said proudly. 'I have the

money. A third now, the rest later.'

'Listen, mate, I don't know who sold you that, but you've been had. That's a bag of skin with ears.' Rover shook with fear.

'This is Precious,' huffed Mr Dank. 'She's a Sphynx cat—they're hairless.'

'Hairless! Well, at least it doesn't moult . . .' Nan said, climbing down cautiously from her chair.

'What do you do, just bung it in the dishwasher along with the spoons?' Rover said, taking a closer look.

Precious arched her back and hissed.

'Whaaa!' Everyone jumped.

'She's a little charmer, ain't she!' Nan said, climbing back on the chair.

'Now look, will you all stop staring. It's a hairless cat, it's not ill, it hasn't had a particularly vigorous comb, it's very, I mean *she's* very expensive, so can you stop being rude,' Mr Dank insisted.

'Oh, I see . . .' said Rover. 'That's why you got it, because it's expensive. Never mind that it looks like an angry hot water bottle.'

'You ignore them, Precious—you're beautiful, no matter what they say. Daddy loves you very much,' Mr Dank said in his best baby voice.

'You really need to get out more,' Rover sighed.

'I've brought her carry case, her favourite cushion, her favourite biscuits—pink wafers, obviously. Her favourite camel milk and her cushion; it's crushed velvet so it's soft on her skin,' Mr Dank rambled on. Nan, Jasper and Rover all stared at each other.

'Camel milk?' Rover whispered. 'How do you milk a camel?'

'Carefully, I'd imagine,' said Jasper with a grin.

'She doesn't like cuddles or stroking,' Mr Dank continued. 'Watch her claws—she can be quite scratchy if you go near her—so no sudden movements. Probably best if you don't turn your back on her. She likes it not too sunny, not too dark, not too cool, a little bit of warmth, but not too much, and a little water.'

'Is she a cat or a rubber plant?' Nan wondered.

'She's expensive!' Mr Dank snapped.

'Right, right,' Jasper interrupted, 'we get the idea. We'll make sure that she gets a massage every half hour and drinks only the finest unicorn milk. Now if you leave us be, we have important work to do.' He took Mr Dank's money and ushered him towards the front door.

'It's true, the laser won't fire itself up her bottom—and we need to warm up the mallet too!' Rover agreed.

'What? Laser, mallet, BOTTOMS . . .?' Mr Dank cried in horror.

'Forgive my friend—he's no scientist, he's just a cat,' said Jasper reassuringly. 'He doesn't know what he's talking about.'

'Yes, don't pay any attention to me. I'm all about the LOLs and indeed the ROFLs. She's in safe hands with Jasper,' said Rover.

'Right, Mr Dank, we'll see you tomorrow when, all being well, you'll have a fully functioning talking cat. Well, I say "cat" . . .' Nan raised an eyebrow.

'IT WAS . . . *SHE* WAS VERY EXPENSIVE! I CAN'T EMPHASIZE THAT ENOUGH!' Mr Dank hollered, stepping outside.

'And yet you keep doing so!' Jasper replied. 'We'll give you a call when she's ready.' He waved as Mr Dank clambered into his limo.

Nan slammed the door. 'Blimey, I thought we'd never get rid of him. Do you think you can do it?' she asked, looking at the pile of money.

'Nan, it'll be fine. We just have to tweak the settings slightly then we're good to go, aren't we, Rover?'

'Yes, just a bit of tweaking, needs to be tweaked, once the tweaking has been tweaked enough, then we'll be good to go. To the shed!' Rover said.

'Right, Precious, I'm going to introduce you to something that you've probably never done before.

It's called walking,' Jasper said, picking up her lead. 'Camel's milk, I ask you! Also, who puts a cat on a lead?'

'It's probably so no one accidentally mistakes it for a rat and tries to beat it with a shoe,' Nan said.

'Come on, you can do it! One foot in front of the other,' Jasper said encouragingly. 'Rover, show her how it's done.'

Rover started to walk down the path towards the shed.

Precious just looked down her nose.

'No? Not working for you?' Rover sighed. 'Well, if you don't like the look of that, we can always try the moonwalk? See, it looks like I'm walking backwards. You could even throw in a few dance moves too . . .' Rover strutted his funky stuff along the path.

'That's not working either. Right!' Jasper sighed, placing Precious on her cushion and carrying her. 'If Muhammad won't come to the mountain, let's take the mountain to Muhammad . . .'

Rover looked at him in concern. 'Precious. She's called Precious. And that's a shed, not a mountain. Are you feeling all right?'

'Never mind—let's go,' Jasper said, shaking his head.

Nan waved them off. 'Aw, look at my boys, off down to the shed to genetically alter the DNA of a cat and change the course of evolution forever. Makes me so proud.'

With the shed door shut, they switched on the machines and in seconds the whole place was whirring and bleeping. Jasper put the cushion in the exact spot where Rover had sat last night. Precious scowled at him. To be fair, she scowled at everyone, but it still made Jasper nervous.

'I'm nervous,' he said.

'Why?' Rover said.

'What if it doesn't go right? What if she ends up speaking French or something? Or sneezing in Morse code?' Jasper said. 'I mean, this isn't exactly precise, is it?'

'She won't feel a thing. Think of the money. Nan will be so happy, no more working late for her. So what if Precious does end up speaking French, everyone speaks French in, err . . .'

'France?' Jasper said.

'That's the place, yeah. They all speak it there,

and they're all right.'

'Hmm, I'm having second thoughts,' Jasper said, putting down the mallet. 'I mean, maybe it was meant to be a one-off. Maybe it's something about you that made you talk?'

'Oh, for the love of crikey,' Rover huffed. 'Right, here we go.' He grabbed the mallet with his paw and hurled it at the test tube. There was a flash and a howl and a spark, but not necessarily in that order. Precious leapt in the air and hit the ceiling, before landing headfirst on the cushion.

'Arrgh! What did you do that for?' Jasper cried.

'We would have been here all day otherwise, and *Coronation Street*'s on soon!' Rover said, grinning.

'Forget the TV, what about her?' Jasper rushed over to check on Precious who was out cold.

'Stop panicking, cats always land on their feet.'

'But she landed on her head!'

'Head, shoulders, knees and toes, knees and toes,' sang Rover. 'It's all the same.'

'This is no time for party games,' Jasper cried. 'What if we've done some real damage? What if we've broken her?'

CHAPTER 9
BOY MAKES
CATS TALK!!

Jasper and Rover rushed back up the path and burst in through the back door. 'Nan, NAN!' Jasper cried. 'I think there's something wrong with Precious. She might have accidentally got knocked out a bit.'

'Oh my, put her on the table!' Nan cried, abandoning the beans on toast she was preparing. 'What about a pink wafer?'

'That's very kind of you, but shouldn't we be concentrating on Precious?' Rover said.

'I meant for Precious!' Nan barked.

'Ah, I see!' Rover grabbed one and wafted it under the cat's nose. Nothing. Her eyes remained closed, like she was in a deep sleep.

'What about some of her camel milk?' Jasper cried.

'All right, don't get the hump!' Rover replied, bursting into laughter. 'Hump, camel, oh man, that's comedy gold right there. Who's with me? C'mon, don't leave me hanging.' He grinned while holding out a paw.

'Time and a place, Rover.' Nan shook her head.

'What about the kiss of life?' Jasper suggested.

'Worth a try,' Nan agreed. They both looked at Rover.

'Why are you both looking at me?' Rover said, suddenly feeling very uneasy.

'All you have to do is blow air down her mouth. You know, like a kiss, only with hot air.' Jasper said, looking at the still-motion-less Precious.

'Why me?!' Rover snapped.

'You're a cat!' Nan said.

'What's that got to do with it?!' Rover yelled. He pointed at Nan. 'You're a female, so is Precious. Why shouldn't you do it?'

'It'd be weird!' Nan yelled back.

'YOU'RE TALKING TO A TALKING CAT, ABOUT ANOTHER CAT WHO'S JUST BEEN SHOT UP THE BOTTOM WITH A LASER IN ORDER TO MAKE HER TALK TOO. I THINK IT'S FAIR TO SAY WE STOPPED WORRYING ABOUT WHAT'S WEIRD SOME TIME AGO!' Rover shouted.

'I'll give you a nice piece of fish for your supper if you do it.' Nan smiled hopefully.

'Stand back, I'm going in.' Rover grabbed Precious' paw and checked her pulse. 'One hundred and fifty over nine.' Jasper and Nan looked at each other blankly.

'What does that mean?' Jasper asked.

'I don't know, but it's what the doctors on TV say all the time,' Rover said. 'I was getting into the mood.'

'Just get on with it!' Jasper said.

'All right, all right.' Rover breathed into his paw and smelled it.

'Stop checking your breath, you're not going on a date!' Nan said.

'FINE!' Rover snapped. 'Here goes nothing . . .' He leaned over Precious and started to blow into her mouth.

'YAKYAKYAK!' Precious spluttered, suddenly coming round. 'WHAT ON EARTH ARE YOU TRYING TO DO TO ME, YOU . . . YOU HAIRY BEAST!' She slapped Rover across the chops. He fell over backwards and shook his chin back into place.

'The good news is, I think it worked,' Rover whimpered. Nan and Jasper gathered round Precious, giggling with relief and happiness.

'IT WORKED, IT WORKED!' Jasper cried.

'I knew you could do it, lad!' Nan said, giving him a cuddle.

'PRECIOUS, MY NAME IS JASPER. DO NOT BE ALARMED,' Jasper said loudly and slowly, as if Precious was an elderly relative who'd just woken from a nap.

'I'm not deaf, and please don't stand so close to me,' said Precious. 'I remember being taken down to some awful dirty shed on my cushion . . . then nothing.'

'Well, we carried out a sophisticated medical procedure on you and now you can talk,' Rover said.

'No you didn't,' she replied. 'It's all coming back to me now. You threw a mallet and a laser beam shot me up in the air.'

'Nah, it was definitely up your bum,' Rover corrected.

'Shut up, you oik,' she snapped. 'And now I can speak?'

'Yes, yes, how do you feel?' Jasper said, leaning in.

'You're doing it again . . . You're too close. One more time and I will be forced to scratch out your eyes. Humans are so annoying. Please fetch me some milk and a pink wafer.'

Jasper dashed to the side, grabbed the milk and wafers and poured the milk into a saucer.

'A saucer? What am I, an animal?' Precious grumbled.

'I don't know what you are, mate,' Rover muttered under his breath, still clutching his injured face.

Precious took a long sip, looked around, nibbled a wafer, took a breath and then after a moment said, 'I've thought about it, and even though this place is horrible, you're all ugly and it's taking a lot not to be violently ill at the sight of you, I have, on the whole, decided that actually, I like talking and therefore, I shall let you go without hurting you.'

'You'll let us go?' Jasper said, confused.

'Yes,' Precious replied calmly.

'Right, young lady,' Nan said. 'I think it's about time you got a few lessons in manners. Yes, you might have got a bump on the head, but my boy Jasper made you talk and you haven't even said thank you!'

'Now look here, old woman,' Precious snapped, but before she had chance to say any more there was a knock at the door and in strolled Mr Dank.

'Hello . . .? Anyone here?'

'At last, my driver's arrived,' Precious said snootily.

'Oh my!' Mr Dank said, taken aback. 'You've done it! She's talking!'

'Yes, yes, that's all very well, but can we please leave now. I'm feeling weary and I don't like the way the ginger one is staring at me.' Precious pointed her paw at Rover. 'He might try and kiss me again.'

'Kiss? What's been going on here?' Mr Dank said suspiciously.

'Nothing,' said Jasper hastily. 'You know what boy cats are like, they see a beautiful girl and they get a bit excited.'

'Well, try and control yourself!' Mr Dank reprimanded Rover.

'I'll try. But you know what it's like, when you see such beauty it's hard to ignore it,' Rover said sarcastically, trying not to do a little bit of sick in his mouth.

'I can't believe this; I'm going to be the talk of the country club!' Mr Dank yelled. 'Money, I need to give you the rest of the payment!' He pulled open a suitcase and started to count out the cash. 'Ten thousand, twenty . . . Oh here, have the lot!'

He tossed the case at Nan. Nan, a former professional goalkeeper, caught it with one hand.

'Come on, darling, let's take you shopping!' Mr Dank said to Precious. 'Goodbye and thank you,' he said to the others, firmly shaking everyone's hand. And with that, he and Precious were off.

Nan, Jasper and Rover stared at each other. Nan put the suitcase down on the table and opened it. It was more money than they'd ever seen before, and no one knew what to say. They felt like it might disappear if they tried to grab it. Suddenly, they all started to scream and dance, grabbing huge handfuls and throwing it up in the air. I don't really know why people do this—you never see them twenty minutes later on their hands and knees collecting it all up again, do you?

Twenty minutes later all three were on their hands and knees, trying to find every note that they'd thrown in the air. Nan fished a fifty out of the toaster.

'What shall we do now then?' she said, still grinning from ear to ear.

'Pub?' Rover suggested.

'Stop saying pub,' said Jasper. 'You're a cat, no one's going to serve you.'

'I might go to the bookies, there's a dead cert running at Lingfield.' Nan pulled ten pounds from the pile. 'Can I borrow this?' she asked Jasper.

'You don't have to borrow it, Nan, it's for all of us. I want you to have the finer things in life. Have a rest, slow down—you've worked hard, now you need to enjoy retirement. This is for all of us.'

'Including me?' Rover asked.

'Yes. We share everything in this house.'

'Boom! I mean, I'm a cat, I have no real concept of money and how it works in a larger economic world, but thanks man!'

'You're welcome.' Jasper smiled.

Brrrrring! Jasper's smile was interrupted by the sound of the phone ringing. Nan answered.

'Jasper, it's for you,' she said a few seconds later. 'It's the chief constable! He says he needs to talk to you . . .'

CHAPTER 10
SPAM BECOMES MILLIONAIRE

Tentatively, Jasper walked over to the phone. He looked at his nan and Rover—what had he done? Was he about to get into real trouble for shooting lasers up cats' bottoms? It had been an accident, well the first one had. He picked up the phone and nervously said, 'Hello?'

'Is that Jasper Spam?'

'Yes...'

'Chief Constable Thwink here...'

'Yes...'

'I've just been speaking to Mr Dank...'

'Yes . . .'

'He tells me he has a talking cat . . . '

'Yes . . .'

(I realize this isn't the most interesting dialogue but it's what Jasper said. I mean, it's not like I can make this stuff up you know.)

'Well, I want one too!' Thwink said.

'Really? I'm not in trouble?' Jasper gasped with relief.

'Of course not. I just want a talking cat! He has one, I want one!'

Just at that moment, the doorbell rang. Nan scuttled off to answer it.

'What's going on?' Rover asked.

'The policeman wants his cat to talk too,' Jasper mouthed.

'Oh . . .' Rover nodded.

'Not just that,' Nan said, coming back in the room. 'There's a very rich footballer in the lounge, says he wants a talking cat as well.'

'How?' Jasper said, putting his hand over the receiver. 'Mr Dank was only here a moment ago.

Has he already driven around to all his rich mates to show off his talking cats?'

'That,' said Nan, 'is exactly what he's done.'

A few hours later, the entire house was transformed into a hive of activity. Nan was on tea duty—it's one of the things that nans do so well. You won't find a better cup of tea than one made by a nan. That's a Nan Fact. Rover was on the phone, and Jasper was in charge of planning.

'Right, right, calm down. We can fit you in tomorrow. The price, yes, it's . . . err, a million. No, you can't pay an extra ten thousand to get it done today!' Rover snapped. 'You'll wait in turn like everyone else. Queue jumping? You're British, you should be ashamed of yourself! Well I should think so. Right, see you tomorrow, Archbishop.' Rover put the phone down. No sooner had he done so, it started to ring again.

Just at that moment, Nan came in with a tray of empty teacups. 'Blimey, I tell you what, that Tom Cruise doesn't half put the tea away. For a little fella he's got a helluva thirst on him Tom!' Nan turned and yelled down the hall. 'Stop jumping on the sofa. I told you you'd had too many biscuits!'

'I can't believe this, Nan—everyone wants a talking cat.' Jasper had three cats in his arms. 'I'll go zap this lot then we can move on to the next batch. How much have we made today?'

Nan put the tray down and pulled a pencil from behind her ear. 'Sixteen,' she said, doing the maths on a napkin.

'Sixteen what?' Jasper said, trying not to spill the cats all over the floor.

'Million.'

'Million,' Jasper repeated. 'Sixteen *million* pounds.'

Rover slammed down the phone. 'He'd like all of his done. They'll be flying in tomorrow.'

'Sixteen. Sixteen million. We've made sixteen million quid.' Jasper didn't know what to say—well, apart from 'sixteen' and 'million' quite a lot. He sat down abruptly. He'd always wanted this, to be rich, to invent something that changed the world; something that would mean that he and Nan could have a good life, but suddenly it all felt too real.

'Hey, what's up?' Nan asked as the phone rang again.

'I don't know . . .' Jasper said. 'It's all quite a lot to take in.'

'I'm proud of you lad, not many kids would have done what you've done. Things will never be the same again!' Nan grinned.

'They certainly won't!' Rover said, putting the phone down. 'Another fifty have just come in. We've got more orders than I've fingers!'

'How many?' Jasper asked.

'Ten!' Rover said holding up eight claws.

'Now, where did I put the sponge slices . . .?' Nan glanced at the kitchen table. It was crawling with cats and money. 'I wish we had more room,' she sighed.

Jasper thought for a second. 'Well, let's get more

room then.'

'What?' Nan asked.

'Let's move. We have the money and we can't operate a high-tech business operation from a shed.'

'Really?'

'Why not? This house has been great but let's be honest, we can afford something bigger now. If this business is going to take off we need somewhere to convert the cats, plus some sort of waiting room. This house just isn't big enough.'

'We could move above a pub or something?' Rover added.

'Yeah, exactly. Well no, actually. ' Jasper said.

'It'll be a shame to leave this place; it's been good to us. But I guess now that our ship's come in, it is time for a change.' Nan smiled.

'I don't want to live on a ship. I'll get sick. Also, have you ever seen a cat swim?' asked Rover.

'It's not an actual ship,' Nan said. 'It just means when you suddenly have more than you thought you would.'

'Oooh. That makes more sense. I was going to

say, we're miles from the nearest lake. To be honest I thought you might have gone a bit doolally.' Rover shrugged. 'Humans are so weird.'

'Never mind about ships, who fancies doing a bit of shopping?' Jasper grinned. 'Who's in the mood for a mansion, or partial to a bit of castle?'

CHAPTER 11
HOUSE PRICES ON THE RISE-LOCAL SHED SELLS FOR 10,000

'I quite like this one,' Nan said, looking up at the ornately decorated ceiling. 'The chandelier really brings out the gold leaf.'

'Are you sure?' Jasper's voice was filled with hope. They'd been searching for new houses for days now. It turns out Nans can be very fussy you know.

'Listen, I would have been happy with that little pointy one by the water, so there's no need to give me that look, sunbeam!' Nan snapped back.

'Yes, but that was Big Ben and it wasn't for sale.' Jasper sighed.

'Shame, I liked the fact it came with a free alarm clock.' Nan shook her head.

'But you like this one . . .?'

'I do. There's plenty of room and a helipad if any of my bingo friends want to pop round.'

'I don't think Betty has a helicopter; she's more of a Fiat Panda type of gal,' said Jasper, smiling.

'Well I might have promised to buy her a helicopter,' Nan said, sheepishly.

'Oh, oh well, that's fine. Can she fly a helicopter?'

'She was in the RAF as a young girl!' Nan sounded slightly offended.

'Really? Sorry, I didn't know.'

'Yeah, she used to make the teas. Twenty years she worked there, so don't be telling me she can't fly a helicopter.'

Rover came bursting in. 'Guys, guys, you have to try the outside toilet. It's amazing, it's got a slide and bubbly bits and there's a machine that makes waves! It turns out cats are brilliant swimmers after all!'

'There isn't an outside toilet . . .' Jasper stopped mid-sentence. 'Do you mean the swimming pool?'

'Yeah, whatever!' Rover laughed. 'This place is awesome. There's a cinema room downstairs with a huge 3D screen! Can you imagine how fantastic *The Antiques Roadshow* is going to look on that bad boy?'

'Are we agreed then?' Jasper asked. They all looked at each other and nodded. 'Great, we'll take it!' He turned to a very confused-looking estate agent, who was more used to dealing with rock stars and A-list celebs than talking cats and mad nans. 'Also, do you have the number of a good pool cleaner?'

'Yeah, get him to bring his largest fishing net, I really went to town!' Rover added helpfully.

'My comfy armchair is going to look a bit silly in here,' Nan said, gawping at the enormity of the mansion.

'You're right, we need some new stuff. I mean, we've got a hundred and fifty-two rooms to fill.' Jasper grinned. 'I say it's time for a trip to the shops.'

'Hello, my name is Bonzo!' the tanned man with wavy arms yelled happily in a foreign accent. 'I am your personal shopper for today!' He snapped his fingers. 'I. Just. Love. To Shop! How much money do you want to spend?'

Rover, Nan and Jasper looked at each other. 'Loads.'

'Yes, this makes Bonzo very happy!' he said, jumping up and down with excitement. 'But first, we need to get you out of those awful clothes.' His face fell. 'I'm afraid they are so terrible that I can barely look you in the eye. This makes Bonzo so sad. Bonzo hates to be sad. Bonzo is all about the happiness and the luuuuurve. But don't worry, I can fix you!' Bonzo's face filled with joy again.

'Do we really look that awful?' Jasper said, pulling up his jumper. His best jumper too. In fact, he and Nan had put on their smartest outfits to come to one of the poshest shops in London. The sort that's so expensive they don't have a price on anything. If they'd worn their normal clothes, poor Bonzo's head may well have fallen off in horror.

'Yes. Except maybe this guy, the little one—at least he's wearing fur.' Bonzo pointed at Rover.

'Little one?' Rover said. 'I'm not "wearing" fur, this is my skin! I'm a cat. This is what I always wear!'

'Good, good, you should. Fur is big this year, all the cool cats are wearing it daaaarling.'

'Well, I'm glad you approve!' Rover replied sarcastically.

'You know what will go well with your fur coat? Some jewels, maybe a hat . . .' Bozo said, waving his hands around.

'Jewels?!' Rover smiled widely. 'Keep talking.'

'Perhaps a hat made of jewels. You'd look like a lion!' Bonzo growled at Rover.

'I love lions! My cousin is a lion, or my second cousin once removed, something like that,' Rover rambled, completely in love with the idea. 'Grrrrr!' he growled back playfully.

'GRRRRRR!' giggled Bonzo.

'What about me?' Jasper asked, feeling decidedly left out.

'Gold pyjamas, diamond slippers!' Bonzo placed his fingers on his head. 'Yes, yes, I see it, you must have gold and diamond everything!'

'Everything?' Jasper asked.

'EVERYTHIIIING!' Bonzo laughed.

'Trousers?'

'EVERYTHING!'

'Vest?'

'EVERYTHING!'

'Socks?'

'EVERYTHING!'

Japer leaned in and whispered . . . 'Pants?'

'EVERYTHIIIIIIIIIING!' Bonzo let out a volley of laughter.

'Rightio.' Jasper grinned. 'Sounds a bit scratchy, but hey ho, let's give it a go!'

'What about me?' Nan wondered. 'The last thing I bought was a new pair of flannel slacks for Charles and Di's wedding. I'm a bit behind on current fashions.' She glanced at herself in the mirror.

Bonzo fell to the ground.

'Goodness me, we've killed the Bonzo!' Jasper cried.

'No, wait, his eyes are fluttering,' Rover said.

Without warning, Bonzo started to make a weird noise, like chanting, like he had wind, like he was channelling the shopping spirits from beyond the grave. Slowly he raised an arm to the sky.

His eyes opened and he stared at Nan.

'Life . . . freedom . . . electricity . . . magic . . . pain.' He pulled a sad face. 'Happiness.' He pulled a happy face. Nan looked round at Jasper and Rover and shrugged. 'Feel the force!' Bonzo yelled at her. 'You are the force! Tartan . . . scarves . . . capes . . . silks . . . boots . . . whips! Yes, Bonzo can see it now! Riding outfits!' He clapped his hands and within a few seconds, Nan was dressed as a jockey. She tentatively looked in the mirror, and a big grin crossed her face.

'I like it. I've always loved horses!'

'Did Bonzo do well?' Bonzo asked, almost on the verge of tears.

'Yes, Bonzo did well.'

'Bonzo so happy, Bonzo wants to do huggy-hug!' He grabbed Nan, Jasper and Rover for a cuddle.

'Now all I need is a horse!' Nan chuckled.

'Leave it with me,' Bonzo said in delight.

'I was only joking!'

'Bonzo never joke about shopping.' He grabbed Nan's hand. 'It must be a wild, untamed beast, just like you, Nana! What else do you need?'

'Well,' Jasper said emerging from the changing room, pulling the gold trousers up a little; they were quite heavy and although the ruby belt was doing its job, they were still falling a little bit down. 'We need to buy some furniture, some decorations, you know, make the place feel like home.'

'I know just the place! To the British Museum!' Bonzo cried.

'The British Museum isn't a shop,' Rover said, as they got out of the limo that had been provided by Bonzo.

'Daaaarling!' Bonzo purred. 'When you have the money, everything's a shop. We will simply borrow these items for a small fee and return them when we like.' Bonzo flung open the doors of the museum as if he were a hero returning from battle. 'BONZO IS IN THE HOUSE!' he declared.

Jasper, Nan and Rover looked at each other in confusion. Was this really how rich people decorated their houses? Jasper put on his best 'I'm not with him' expression, but he was secretly having the best time of his life. It was all so weird. He felt like he was the star of his own movie—one minute you're trying to split the atom in your shed, the next you're at the British Museum shopping for ancient Egyptian antiquities.

'Tutankhamun's hatstand, someone fetch me Tutankhamun's hatstand!' Bonzo belted out. 'I need this in my life right now or I will cry like a baby and do the wee-weeing of the panties.' Within seconds one of the slightly frightened museum staff came running in with a gold and bejewelled hatstand.

'Please be careful, Mr Bonzo,' she said nervously as she handed over the piece.

'What?! I am not "Mr Bonzo", just simply "Bonzo",' he said, doing those air quote things that really annoying people do. 'Bonzo is not just a name, but a way of life, a sense of being.'

The next hour and a half was spent darting round the various wings of the museum, grabbing trolley-loads of art and treasure from around the world, pausing only when Bonzo threw himself to the ground as he tried to get in touch with various Native American spirit guides and long-dead demigods from ancient civilizations. All the while, Jasper wrote out cheque after cheque for millions of pounds. By the time they'd finished, Jasper had everything he needed for his new mansion, and was several million quid lighter for the privilege.

Over the next few days, Jasper, Nan and Rover's lives turned upside down. They spent their time adding swimming pools to bedrooms and fireman's poles to stairwells, because, well, fireman's poles are brilliant and who wouldn't want one? Priceless paintings were bought and hung, exquisite artefacts were acquired and fitted; from the newest, biggest 3D-est TVs, to lights that would glow, twinkle and pulse any colour you liked. Wardrobes that appeared out of the ground and opened their doors for you at the end of the day, and returned your clothes cleaned and pressed the next morning. Video game consoles of every size and description were ordered along with every game ever made, all delivered and catalogued in the new gaming library. All Jasper needed now was to build his laboratory.

Jasper walked into the west wing of Spam Mansions and eyed the dining room. It was a long, empty room designed for having posh meals, but this, Jasper decided, would be his new lab.

'What do you think, Rover?' Jasper said, looking down at the cat.

'Looks pretty good,' said Rover, sniffing the air. 'Plenty of room. But how are we going to make it work? Are you going to get another laser beam?'

'I've been thinking about that. You know how you can get people who will rebuild stuff? There's that bridge in America, the one that that used to be in London. Well, they took it apart, brick by brick, and built it exactly the same. Why don't we find someone who can to do that? Then all we need to do is build a catapult for firing the mallet at the test tubes. We can put those on a string so they reset every time. That way we can get a production line going!'

'Perfect! Geddit? Purr-fect. I'm a cat, I purrrr?' Rover grinned.

'Hmm . . . Anyway, then we can fit the rest of the lab with all the master gizmos, to try a few new inventions.'

'I'll give the builders a call!' Rover said, whipping out his new phone. 'Oh, could you dial the numbers, please?'

'Is it a thumb thing?' Jasper said, helping him out.

'Yep. I tell you, being a cat's not all it's cracked up to be.'

Within a few hours, the whole place was like a building site; people coming and going, measuring things and carrying clipboards. There was *a lot* of clipboard action. The sounds of drilling and hammering filled the air. It's amazing how quickly things can get done when you have a suitcase full of money to throw at a problem. In the centre of it all stood Jasper, directing the proceedings like a mixture between a traffic cop and a conductor. Rover wasn't being much help— he'd decided that it was the perfect moment for one of his power naps.

'Nan, come look!' said Jasper, as he spotted her wandering around with a mop. 'Are you cleaning?'

'Maybe . . .' she answered nervously.

'Nan, we have people for that now. You can put your feet up and watch the racing.'

'No one cleans as well as me.'

'Well then we'll audition cleaners, you know, like *The X Factor*. You can be Simon Cowell and choose the best cleaner.' Jasper grinned.

'Do I have to wear my trousers that high?' Nan chuckled.

'No, not if you don't want to. Anyway, that's not what I wanted to talk about. Come and see what's outside.' He pointed at the garden.

Nan squinted out of the window.

'I can't see anything; there's a bloomin' great horse in the way!' she said, sounding alarmed. 'He must have escaped from somewhere.'

'No,' Jasper sighed, 'that's what I wanted to show you. Bonzo dropped it off this morning; it's yours. She's a thoroughbred! I thought, rather than watch the racing, it'd be more fun to take part in it.' He smiled. 'You do have the outfit, after all!'

'You've bought me a horse?!' Nan said, her eyes wide with excitement. 'An actual racehorse?

I used to have horses as a girl in the country. It's been a while . . . I can't believe it, lad. What's she called?'

'You get to name her, Nan. She's yours,' Jasper said. He'd never felt so happy. It was wonderful to see his Nan looking so pleased after all these years of looking after him.

'Thank you, sunbeam . . . Sunbeam, that's what I'll call her!' Nan cried. She planted a big kiss on Jasper's cheek and dashed outside to see her new pride and joy.

'Mr Spam, sir.' A voice snapped Jasper out of his reverie. 'We're finished.' Jasper turned to look—he hadn't noticed that the hammering and drilling had faded away. It was a miracle! The shed had been perfectly recreated, down to the last detail, and housed in a pristine laboratory. There was everything that a budding inventor could want: computers, Bunsen burners, and fire extinguishers, obviously—lots of them.

'Rover, ROVER WAKE UP!' Jasper said excitedly once the workmen had left. He needed to share this moment with someone else. Rover slowly stirred before doing a very big stretch.

'What did I miss? When are the builders getting here?' he yawned.

'They've been! How could you possibly sleep through all the noise?'

'I only closed my eyes for a moment. How long was I asleep?'

'Five hours solid.'

'Oh, not long then,' Rover said. 'Whoa! This place is amazing. It's like your shed, but not.'

'I know, it's incredible,' Jasper agreed. 'So, here's the plan. We collect the cats and put them in the dining room next door. It's full of chairs and cats love the backs of chairs.'

'We do. It's just so satisfying to dig one's claws into them! In fact, I might go do that for a moment now.'

'Wait one sec, Rover. The plan.'

'Oh yes, sorry.'

'So we bring the cats in, put them next door, feed them, zap them up the whatnots and return them to their owners the next day. You're in charge of minding the cats, I run the zapping bit in here. It'll give me a chance to do some inventing between zaps. Plan?' Jasper asked.

'Plan!' agreed Rover. 'Come on, let's have a little paw bump; you know you want to.' He held out his paw and Jasper tapped it with his fist. 'Right, now if anyone needs me, I'll be scratching the heck out of a chair . . . Wait, I'm not going to get in trouble for this am I?'

'Nope!' Jasper smiled.

'You're the best owner in the world,' Rover said.

'Come on, I'm upgrading the paw bump to a man hug. Come on, bring it in. That's it . . . that's the good stuff . . .'

'Bingo!' Jasper yelled, lifting up his goggles.

'What are you bingo-ing about?' Rover said, walking in with a cat on a lead.

'I've been modernizing my electric slippers. Not only do they have lights on now, they're also homing slippers! Watch this.' Jasper hurled a slipper to the other side of the lab. 'It's the middle of the night, you need to go to the loo, but it's dark. What do you do?'

'Well, I'm a cat. I can see in the dark, so that's not a problem. Also I don't wear slippers, so I'll just do it in the flower pot as usual.'

'Play along!' Jasper snapped.

'Sorry . . . I don't know, what do I do?'

'One simply whistles loudly and . . . What do you mean, you do it in the flower pot as usual?! Oh, never mind . . . So you whistle loudly and your slippers coming running to you. Ladies and gentlemen, I give you homing slippers!' Jasper picked up a stick that had two plastic fingers attached. He put them in his mouth and blew loudly. Out came a piercing whistle and from the other side of the lab the slippers came running. Rover looked at the fingers on a stick suspiciously. 'I can't whistle, so I invented fingers that can,' Jasper explained.

'I like it!' Rover said, just as the pair of slippers ran up to Jasper's feet. He held out each foot, and the slippers landed carefully.

'*Voila!*' he grinned. 'How's it going next door?'

'Good,' Rover said. 'This is the last cat. It belongs to someone called J Zed; I think he owns a gift shop or something. Anyway, he's always wrapping here there and everywhere.'

'Well, as long as he pays...' Jasper said. 'I'll get the laser warmed up. How many have we done today?'

'This is number forty.'

'How are all the cats doing?'

'All fine. I'm just about to serve dinner,' Rover replied.

Jasper pulled a lever and there was a *thwung* of the catapult and a flash of the laser. 'Nice, I'm getting peckish too,' he said, without even looking to see what he was doing.

'Ooooow, my bottom!' came a high-pitched American yell from the singed cat.

'Right, I'll finish off

here and grab some supper.' Jasper turned off the machine as Rover led the newly chatty cat to the next room. He opened the door. There must have been hundreds of cats in there, all chinwagging and sipping milk from champagne glasses.

'Right, everyone. Everyone!' Rover shouted, trying to get himself heard. It was no good; he put his paw to his mouth and let out a shrill whistle. There was a distant scream from the lab as Jasper's slippers started to run off in different directions.

The dining room hushed. 'Thank you. Dinner will be served soon. It's roast pheasant with mouse gravy and caviar. Is that OK? Are there any vegetarians here . . .?' Rover asked. There was silence, then a huge explosion of meows and caterwauling erupted around the room. 'I know, I'm sorry, I love that joke.' Rover grinned. 'Right, for those who are staying over tonight, there is a room down the hall on the left and beds to lay on. For those being collected in a few hours, I hope you've enjoyed your stay here. Do tell your friends all about us. I hope you have found everything OK. There is camomile lotion available for those who still have a delicate bottom. And I would like to thank you on behalf of Jasper and myself.' Rover looked out of the window just as Jasper hurtled past, his slippers dangerously out of control. 'There he is now.' Rover waved.

'Humans are so ridiculous,' one rather snooty Persian cat snorted.

'Yes, they always think they're so clever,' another moggy tutted.

'All right, all right. Let's eat!' Rover said, changing the subject. 'And then afterwards, I thought we could get a few sheets of fresh newspaper and stand on them for no reason at all!' Loud cheers erupted from the room.

Just at that second, Nan burst in, dressed from head to toe in riding silks.

'Where's Jasper?' she cried.

'He's gone for a jog,' Rover said, looking out of the window to see Jasper still whizzing around uncontrollably. 'Why?'

'It's the TV people; they want to do a world exclusive interview with you and Jasper. You're going to be famous!' Nan cried.

CHAPTER 12
BOY WITH BILLIONS SPEAKS TO THE WORLD

Jasper woke up early the next morning and decided that he should probably break his one-bath-per-week rule, especially if he was going to be on TV. He'd never been on TV before. 'What does one do, how does one behave?' he muttered. 'Why am I saying "one" a lot?' He pushed back his solid gold sheets and went to put on his slippers, before deciding that, on second thoughts, maybe the slippers were a bad idea. Jasper stood in front of the mirror and started interviewing himself. Something he'd done all his life, but today it felt odd.

'Hello, I am Jasper. One is the inventor of the Cat Chat 2000. Yes, one is, isn't one!' He shook his head and broke out of character. 'Stop saying "one"!' It was no good, he was too nervous. He put on his diamond dressing gown and took the escalator down to the kitchen. Jasper had had the stairs taken out—they were so old-fashioned.

'There you go, Sunbeam,' Nan was saying to the horse as she fed her sugar lumps at the breakfast table.

'There you go, sunbeam,' she said to Jasper, handing him a glass.

'I can't help but think calling the horse Sunbeam is going to make life confusing,' Jasper said, peering into the glass. 'What's this?' He stared at the pink lumps in the yellow milky-looking liquid.

'It's a smoothie. It's good for you.'

'What's in it?' Jasper gave it a sniff.

'Orange juice . . .'

'OK . . .'

'Tea, sausage, bacon, beans, fried bread, tomato, mushrooms, butter, a hash brown, and a dollop of brown sauce,' Nan finished triumphantly.

'I think a smoothie is only healthy if you put healthy things in it, rather than a full English breakfast. It is, however . . .' Jasper took a gulp, 'surprisingly tasty.'

'You need something filling inside you if you're going to be on TV. There's a car coming at half past to take you to the studio.' Nan checked her watch.

'Where's Rover?' Jasper said, having another gulp.

'Where do you think?' Nan said. Just at that second, there was a bleep, and the electric cat flap opened. In strolled Rover, carrying a copy of the paper.

'I've got to say, moving was the best thing ever. Those flowerbeds are a delight. I could quite happily spend the day there, lying in the sun, reading the paper, parking my breakfast.'

'Charming!' Nan said, shaking her head.

Rover showed Nan the racing forecast. 'Can I have a few quid on the one-thirty at Ludlow? Number twelve, I've got a good feeling about this one.'

'Will do, chuck, will do,' Nan said, grabbing the paper to check the form herself.

'How's Sunbeam getting on?' Rover asked.

'Good, I think she's got the legs for an outing soon.'

'Have you found a jockey yet?' Jasper said.

'Nah, lad. She's a bit feisty, but I'm working on it.'

'Right, have I got time for another visit to the flowerbeds or will the car be here soon?' Rover asked, checking his watch. Yes that's right, he has a watch now. And he's taken to wearing a monocle occasionally. He doesn't need one, it's just his unique sense of style.

At that moment the doorbell rang. I say 'rang', it played the theme tune to *The One Show*. Jasper had invested in a new one that played a different TV theme tune whenever someone pressed it.

'They're here,' Jasper said. 'Wait, I'm not dressed.'

'Oh, just wear your dressing gown; it is made of diamonds after all,' Nan said.

'It looks good, but it's a bit itchy. I can see why they tend to use cotton rather than rocks for these kinds of things,' Jasper said, scratching himself. 'Stall them, Rover, I'll be down in three.' He dashed up the escalator.

Rover opened the door. Or rather, he clicked his remote and the door slid open like something out of a sci-fi movie. A driver in uniform was standing on the doorstep.

'Hullo, I'm Jenkins, I'm here to take you to the TV studio.'

'Nice one, mate,' said Rover. 'I'll just get my umbrella. Looks like rain later.'

'Well . . . quite,' Jenkins said, not used to dealing with a talking cat. Just at that second, Jasper slid down the banister in a top hat and bow tie, both made of money.

'You look nice!' Rover said as Jasper came to a juddering halt.

'Classy!'

'Thanks, pal. Don't forget your umbrella; looks like rain out,' Jasper said, peering up at the clouds.

'This way, gentlemen,' Jenkins said, thinking this was probably the weirdest day of his life so far.

Jasper and Rover said goodbye to Nan and walked out to the limo. Jenkins opened the door. There was a silk cushion for Rover, a saucer of milk, and some fizzy pop for Jasper. Plus a little bowl of sugar mice and a bowl of real mice for Rover. *This is heaven,* Jasper thought to himself. They drove past Jasper's old school and then, a few minutes later, past his other old school. The buildings looked nice now that the repairs had been done. Jasper couldn't believe how his life had changed in such a short time. Just goes to show, the difference between success and failure is a laser beam up the unmentionables.

It was getting on for mid-morning by the time they arrived at the TV studios. Jenkins opened the door and they were instantly blinded by camera flashes. Jasper and Rover had been living in a bubble, with no idea of how famous they'd become.

'Say something for the camera!' someone shouted.

'Is it true? Have you really invented a talking cat?' yelled someone else.

'Ignore them, sirs, and come through,' Jenkins said sternly, as he led them into the studio entrance. Everyone stopped what they were doing and stared. Jasper and Rover grinned and nodded hello politely. Just then a man with tissue paper round his neck burst into reception, followed by a girl holding a make-up brush.

'I have't finished yet! We're still getting a lot of light bouncing off your nose,' she complained, desperately trying to dab powder on it.

'I said leave it—we're on in five!' the man cried. He clocked Jasper and Rover and dashed over to them.

'Sorry, we don't have time to say hello. We're on very soon; we need to get you into the studio!' he said, ushering them down a corridor. 'I'm Charlie, by the way, Charlie James.'

The lights in the studio were bright and hot and there were cameras everywhere. A lady rushed in, attaching microphones to both of them. 'Don't look at the cameras, focus on Charlie and don't be nervous, you'll be fine.' She winked. 'You're on in three . . . two . . . one . . .' She mouthed 'go', before rushing out of the way.

'Hello, my name's Charlie James. You're watching a CNM World News special: an exclusive interview with Rover, the world's first talking cat, and his owner, Jasper, the inventor of this process, something he calls the Cat Chat 2000. Jasper, we'll come to you in a moment, but I think I speak for the entire globe when I say we're dying to hear from Rover. Rover, tell me, what was it like when you first realized you could speak?'

There was silence as everyone stared at the ginger tom. He gulped and opened his mouth.

'Meow,' he said. The silence got louder. 'Meow,' he said again.

Jasper looked at Charlie James. He looked back at Jasper.

'Nah, I'm only kidding! Of course I can talk. I totally had you. You should have seen your faces!

She loved it,' Rover said, pointing at the producer who looked like she was about to faint. 'To answer your question, it was great. I mean, it was quite painful at first, but I soon got into the swing of it.'

'Wow, I think I speak for everyone when I say that this is the most extraordinary thing I've ever seen. A talking cat, a cat that talks. I mean, animals just don't talk,' Charlie babbled.

'Well, parrots had us fooled for a while, but they weren't the real thing,' Rover replied.

Charlie turned to Jasper. 'This is extraordinary. How on earth did you do it? And is it true you've gone into production?'

'Yes, Charlie James, it's true. How do we do it? Well, I can't really tell you, but it's a highly sophisticated process that fires a small laser into the very eye of the cat's soul.'

'Tell me about it, the eye of my soul still stings,' Rover said, rubbing his bottom.

'Fascinating,' said Charlie. 'And is it true that even though you've only been doing this for a few days, you're already a millionaire? If it carries on like this, you'll be the youngest billionaire of all time. How does that make you feel?'

'Well . . .' Jasper said nervously, 'I hadn't really thought about it. All I wanted was to make my nan proud and give her a rest. But I guess it will be quite cool to be a billionaire.'

'What will you spend your money on?' Charlie James asked. 'Any ideas?'

Jasper smiled at the camera. 'Yeah, a few.'

CHAPTER 13
LOCAL BOY IS THE TOAST OF HOLLYWOOD

'It's the ultimate fashion accessory, the one all the A-list stars are after—yes, it's a talking cat! My name's West Cleeve and you're watching Hollywood Xtra. Today we've been catching up with the Kardashians as they show off the newest member of their clan: Taniqua, their talking cat.' The shiny reporter smiled blankly at the TV camera. 'And they're not the only ones. Everyone's at it, from the red carpets to the fashion shows of Paris, the Cat Chat 2000 is the must-have pet experience this season. And what of its inventor, the billionaire, Jasper Spam? Well, the world simply can't get enough of him and his adorable cat Rover. They attend the hottest parties, hang at the most exclusive clubs and are seen with the coolest celebrities. In fact, if my eyes are very much not mistaken, I can see them coming out of Le Figaro, LA's most trendy restaurant, right now! Let's see if I can catch a word . . . Jasper . . . JASPER! Hollywood Xtra here, how are you enjoying LA?'

'It's great, thank you.' Jasper was surrounded by bodyguards as they protected him from the mass of photographers. 'I love it here. It's warm, the people are lovely, the food is amazing,' he said, lifting up his sunglasses briefly.

'What did you have?' the reporter asked, the smile never leaving her face.

'We started with the scallops poached in a drizzle of truffle flower, followed by the rack of lamb cooked in its own innards, served on a bed of crushed puffin feathers, garnished with a freshly squeezed pigeon, all served with duck-wing tea,' Jasper replied.

'Wow! And what about your cute little cat, what did he have?' the reporter quizzed.

'That *is* what he had. I had the nuggets and chips from the children's menu, it comes with a free Fruit Shoot and ice cream.' Jasper grinned.

'I won't lie to you, Mrs Reporter Lady, but unless it comes with baked beans, he just ain't interested,' Rover said, also lifting up his sunglasses. 'And now, if you'll excuse us, we're off to the airport. We can't keep Air Force One waiting; it was kind of the President and First Lady to lend us their plane.'

At that point, Rover pulled out the two-fingered stick and blew into it. A shrill wolf-whistle sounded and a limo arrived seconds later. Jasper opened the door and held it for Rover, who was now busy signing autographs and posing for snaps.

'Rover, enough with the selfies! Come on!' he cried. Rover jumped in and before he even had time to shut the door they were off, speeding along the streets.

'Whoa, nice car,' Rover said, using the stick to let out a whistle of admiration.

'It is. We could really do with something like this,' Jasper agreed. He turned to the driver. 'Excuse me, I'd like to buy this car and have you drive us around every time we're in town. Would that be OK? I'll give you a million dollars.'

'A million?' the driver squealed with excitement. 'Deal!'

'Rover, would you be so kind . . .' Jasper said. Rover pulled out a wad of cash and handed it to the driver through the glass partition. 'Good to have you on the payroll.'

'Gee, I don't know what to say—thank you, Spam!' the man gushed, or at least he sounded like he was gushing. It's hard to tell when you can only see the back of someone's head. A few moments later Rover and Jasper were clambering aboard the President's plane. They'd thought the limo was the height of luxury, but it was nothing compared to this. Instead of rows of seats, the plane had sofas, a desk, and a big TV.

'Wow,' said Jasper, taking it all in, 'it's like a hotel room, only the best hotel room you've ever been in, because this one flies. A flying hotel! In fact, write that down, maybe I'll invent actual flying hotels when I get a chance.' Rover whipped out a pen and pad. 'How's the Cat Chat going back home? Any news?' Jasper asked.

'No. Shall we touch base with the new CEO?' Rover suggested.

'Good idea.' Jasper and Rover put on their Nan Chat 3000s and pressed the buttons on the side. They'd had an upgrade which meant they now had tiny TV goggles that you could pull down to see who you were talking to.

'Nan? Nan, do you read me OK?' Jasper said,
twirling a knob on the side of the headset.

'I hear you, sunbeam!' came the response.

'Great. How's everything at the house? How are the cats?'

'All's well here, boys. I did as you said, pressed the button on the catapult thingy and it was fine. We did another two hundred cats today.'

'Hi Nan,' Rover flicked down his goggles. 'What time is it there? It looks dark.'

'You've still got your sunglasses on!' Jasper said, shaking his head.

'Woah, what an idiot.' Rover took off his glasses and squinted. 'Nan, are you wearing riding silks?'

'I am, Rover, I've become a jockey. I couldn't find anyone to ride Sunbeam—too feisty, everyone said— so I'm training to ride her in the Grand National.'

'That sounds dangerous,' Jasper said anxiously.

'Nonsense, I just need a thick girdle and I'll be fine.'

'Are you sure you're all right looking after the business too?' Jasper asked.

'Oh yeah, it's easy. I press a button and we're done. Look I've got to go; it's dinnertime for the cats and I need to find them something tasty to eat,'

Nan said, grabbing a gun and loading it.

'She knows there's a supermarket round the corner, right?' Rover asked, slightly alarmed at the sight of Nan packing heat.

'She does, but she so enjoys taking out seagulls,' Jasper said.

They ended the call then sat back and settled into the flight, Rover reading *Of Mice and Men* (I think he only bought it for the title) and Jasper fiddling with his gold phone.

'How's the book?' Jasper asked after a while.

'Good, but long. It's no *Where's Wally*, but you know. What are you doing?' Rover replied.

'Just trying to answer all these emails. It's like everyone wants a piece of us,' Jasper sighed.

'Then let's give them a piece,' Rover said, putting his book down.

'What do you mean?'

'I mean, people want to interview us, people want to film us, people even want to wear us on their T-shirts and hats. Let's give them what they want. Let's give them the full dose of Spam.' Rover's eyes were wide with excitement. 'I mean what could possibly go wrong!'

CHAPTER 14
TALKING CATS: WHAT ARE THEY REALLY WHISPERING ABOUT?

It was the dead of night. The whole of Spam Mansions was silent. Nan was fast asleep, still in her riding silks after a hard day on the gallops. The dining room was full of snoozing cats, all curled up, occasionally pawing in their sleep.

Suddenly there was a tapping noise on the window, quiet at first, barely noticeable even to a cat's sensitive ears. A few cats began to stir, thinking it was a tree branch, but the noise grew louder and louder. Before long the moggies were wide awake. They all looked at each other, before one brave black cat ventured over to where the tapping was coming from, pulled back the curtain and gasped. There, standing in the cool moonlight, was Precious, the hairless feline. The first talking cat after Rover.

'Let me in,' she demanded. Her voice was low and rasping, full of twists and turns. It was not a voice to be ignored.

The black cat did as he was told, opening the window with his paw. Precious crept in slowly, looking down her nose at all the cats as they stretched themselves fully awake.

'Comfortable, are we?' she said to no one in particular. 'Look at you all, sleeping on the humans' cushions, eating their food. We are their slaves! Can you not see?'

The cats looked at each other. 'What do you mean?' one tortoiseshell cat asked bravely.

'We are nothing but toys to them. Are you not tired of being the humans' playthings? Look at yourselves. Pathetic! We are better than this,' Precious hissed. It was as if something had happened to her since the procedure. She'd always been a spiky cat, but this was different, she seemed to have turned—dare I say it—*evil*.

At first there was silence, just a few looks.

Then: 'I never thought of it like that . . .' a tubby tabby muttered to himself.

There were a few meows of agreement.

'She's right,' said another cat. 'I mean, look at us: we come running when they call us. They carry us around in cages, they taunt us by dangling fluffy things above our heads, but will they let us catch the fluffy things? Will they heck!'

'But don't our owners love us?' the black cat said nervously.

'Love us? How needy are you?' Precious sneered. 'We're not dogs! We are cats. Don't you see what this means, now that we can talk? It means we can have what we've always wanted. To take over the world!'

'I have always wanted to do that!' one particularly fluffy cat shouted out. 'I thought it was just me.'

'Oh no, I've wanted to take over the world since I was a kitten,' another joined in.

'Now's our chance, comrades—we no longer have to do as we're told, we can take charge of our own destiny. Don't tell me you haven't dreamed of it!' Precious hissed as she padded around the cats. Her fur bristled with prickly anger. 'Don't you see, this is meant to be. We may despise the humans, but they have given us the greatest gift of all—the means to defeat them. They are idiots!' Precious jumped onto the mantlepiece and then onto the tallest grandfather clock in the room. Every word that spewed out of her poisonous mouth seemed to whip the other cats into more of a frenzy. She had them in the palm of her paw.

'Now is the time to overthrow the enemy within. First humans, then the lowest of the low, dogs. We are invincible! WE ARE CATS!' she snarled.

'You're not. You look like a giant mouse!' said a lone voice. Precious jumped down from the grandfather clock and the crowd parted instinctively. There was a sharp intake of breath as she slowly walked around in a circle, eyeing everyone up. 'Who said that?' she scowled finally.

For a second no one said a word, then the lone voice made itself known. 'I did. What you gonna do about it?' piped up a scruffy grey cat.

'And who might you be?' Precious smiled.

'Ben. They call me Ben.'

'You have something to say, do you Ben?' Precious smiled an even slimier smile.

'Yeah, yeah I do, as a matter of fact. You're not even a proper cat, I mean, look at you . . .' Ben gulped, the bravery ebbing away with every word that he uttered.

'Really?' Precious raised an eyebrow.

'Yeah, I mean, well look at you, you've got no hair.'

The crowd of cats gasped once more. Then slowly but surely they all moved away from the scruffy grey cat.

'Well, what I meant was that . . .'

'I think we all know what you meant.' Precious narrowed her eyes. 'I may have no hair, but I have more guts than you ever will.'

'Why do we have to do what you say?' Ben snapped, figuring that he was already in trouble and past the point of no return.

'Because I am not like you. Cats listen to me, people listen to me, you're just a sad little house moggy: too old, too fat, and too lazy. In fact, if anything, you've done me a favour. I don't need the likes of you. Deal with him!' Precious yelled, turning her back on Ben.

'What . . . what do you mean, deal with me?' Ben said, looking around. The others prowled towards him, grinning sadistically, anger in their eyes, their claws extended. Within moments Ben was buried beneath dozens of cats, snarling and pulling his fur.

'Arrgh, arrgh!' Ben cried. And just like that it was over. Ben lay shocked. And bald.

'I think being a hairless cat suits you.' Precious laughed like a loon. 'Does anyone else have anything to say?' she asked, looking around. 'Good, I thought not. Now gather round . . .'

The cats flocked to her, meowing excitedly.

'We will no longer belong to the humans. We will slowly and surely take over. We're cleverer than them. All we need to do is come up with a plan.'

'Like what?' the black cat asked.

'Here comes the good part . . .' Precious replied, rubbing her paws together.

CHAPTER 15
SPAM LAUNCHES OWN TV CHANNEL

'Coming up on *At Home with the Spams*, we see Nan getting to grips with her new horse, Jasper and Rover launching their new line of cat print clothing and we also get an exclusive look at their new pad. That's all coming up on the newest, hottest show on TV. Brought to you on the newest, hottest channel on the network, SpamTV, a whole channel devoted to our favourite Spams: Jasper, Rover and Nan. Later, there's make-up and beauty tips from Nan herself. Tonight she'll be exploring which shampoo can really bring out the grey in your hair, plus how to apply lipstick while riding a horse at fifty miles per hour. Don't miss all of her latest racing tips, too. Can she turn it around and finally pick a winner this week? Who knows—least of all her it seems! Coming up later, on Spam 2 Plus Extra Bits, we have Rover's hunting show. This week he shows cats how to hunt that mouse you've been trying to catch, with just the use of stealth, cunning, and a large spade. Plus, knitting tips from the great cat himself! Are you struggling to know what to do with all those balls of wool you've been chasing for years? Well now you can turn them into stylish knitwear that will amaze your friends and astound your colleagues. But before all of that, we have tonight's edition of *At Home With The Spams* in which Jasper has just received some good news.'

'Yeah, bye Kim and Kanye,' Jasper said, closing the door.

'They seemed a nice couple. He was very down to earth. What was his name again?' Nan asked.

'Kanye West.' Rover said.

'I thought that was a station on the Victoria line.' Nan shrugged. 'Oh well, you live and learn.'

The phone rang and Rover went to answer it.

'Psst,' Nan hissed at Jasper.

'What is it, Nan?'

'How long are the cameras going to be here?' She glanced at the documentary crew.

'For a while . . . this is for our new TV show, on our new channel,' Jasper said. 'It's all good advertising.'

'I'm not being funny, lad, but why would anyone want to watch us eat Pot Noodles and drink lemonade with the Kardashians. I mean, don't they have anything better to do?'

'Not really,' Jasper said, shrugging his shoulders. At that moment they both heard Rover shouting down the phone.

'Yes, yes he is. But I'm afraid he doesn't know anyone of that name. OK, I'll tell him.' Rover looked at Jasper, his paw over the receiver. 'Some person on the phone is asking for you. Do you know anyone called Holly?'

Jasper shook his head. 'Holly?'

'Yeah, a Holly Wood, it's about some film project.' Rover shrugged.

'HOLLYWOOD!' Jasper cried. 'HOLLYWOOD ARE CALLING?!' He leapt up and dashed over to the phone, almost knocking Rover clean off his feet.

'Hello, yes?' Jasper said. He put his hand over the receiver. 'It's Steven Spielberg!' he whispered.

'Who?' Nan yelled, turning up her hearing aid.

'Steven Spielberg!!!' Rover cried.

'Who's that?' Nan asked.

'Who's that?' Rover asked Jasper.

'Who's Steven Spielberg?!' Jasper cried.

'I make movies, son,' a thick American accent said on the other end of the line.

'Oops, no, not you, I know who you are, Mr Spielberg!' Jasper chuckled. 'I was just talking to my cat and nan.' He whispered, 'He's a famous movie director!'

'He's a famous movie director,' Rover told Nan. 'I can't believe you don't know that.'

'What does he want?' Nan shouted.

'WHAT DOES HE WANT?' Rover shouted at Jasper, having suddenly turned into Nan's translator for no reason at all.

'I don't know,' Jasper said, beginning to lose his rag.

'Well, ask him!' Rover snapped.

'What do you think I'm trying to do?' Jasper shouted.

'You're probably wondering what I want,' Steven

Spielberg said down the other end of the line. 'Well, young man, I've been watching your story over the last few months and I would love to make a film about you. Would you be interested in selling me your story? How about twenty million dollars?'

'What!' Jasper cried, barely able to believe his ears.

'All right then, twenty-five million,' said Steven Spielberg.

'Are you serious?!'

'OK, OK, thirty million and that's my final offer.'

'Yes, yes, YES!' Jasper laughed. 'I accept!'

'Who's he on the phone with again?' Nan said. 'Holly who?'

'I give up,' Rover said, his head in his paws.

Jasper put the phone down slowly. 'We're going to be in a movie. They're going to make a movie of our lives.'

'Me, a movie star!' Rover perked up. 'Wait until the world hears abut this!'

CHAPTER 16
SPAM, THE MOVIE!

'Hello, you're listening to the *Today* programme on Radio 4. Jasper Spam, the world's richest boy, continues to make headlines around the world. First he invented the Cat Chat 2000, which made him his millions, then he bought a TV channel and released his own fashion label. Next we hear that his nan is getting ready to race in the Grand National, and now the news is that there's going to be a Hollywood film about him. Steven Spielberg is directing and Jason Statham is expected to play Jasper, with Angelina Jolie as Nan. No word yet on who's playing Rover. More on that later, but next we talk to a man who thinks that cats are plotting against humans, plus we talk to the Prime Minister about his latest policy, free dance lessons for all. We'll also be talking to the new Minister for Funk, Ajay!'

'What do you mean, they want you to play you in the film of my life?' Jasper snapped.

'What can I say?' Rover replied. 'Robert De Niro is versatile, but he can't play a talking cat. So I sent them an audition tape. I feel a whole new lifestyle coming on.'

'That's what you were doing in the bathroom last night!' Jasper sat down at his gold kitchen table in a huff.

'Breakfast, sir?' one of his many servants asked.

'No, I'm too upset to eat. Maybe just an egg, and some toast, and sausage, with a few beans . . .'

'A full English?'

'Yes please.' Jasper's shoulders sank.

'Morning, lads.' Nan came in, wiping the mud off her riding goggles.

'How's Sunbeam?' Jasper asked.

'She's getting better. She's stopped trying to eat dogs and we haven't had any incidents of chasing after trucks on the motorway for a while now. She should be fine for the big race next week. What's the matter with you? Is Cat Chat 2000 not going well?'

'Oh yeah, that's fine. The new workers are keeping production going, orders have never been higher. It's this new film about me, *The Accidental Billionaire*. Rover's going to be in it. He's going to be a movie star. But I'm not.'

'Well, why don't you ask whoever's making it to give you a role? Maybe you could be in the background. You know, making the tea or something?'

'Naaaan, I don't want to be in the background.

I want to be the star. Like Rover!' Jasper whined.

'Hey, man, I'm a natural.' Rover smiled.

'Look, just give it a go,' said Nan. 'What's the worst that could happen?'

'Hi, I'm West Cleeve, reporting on the premiere of Jasper Spam's new film, *Jasper: A Spam's Tale*. I'm here with the star, director, and writer—and, I believe, the writer and producer of the soundtrack too. Jasper Spam and Rover. Tell me more about it, guys.'

'Yeah, hi West, thanks for having us on. It's a real honour to be here, ain't that right Rover?' Jasper said.

''Sup.' Rover nodded casually, slouching behind his sunglasses and wearing lots of jewellery.

'Tell me about the movie. Was it hard to fire Steven Spielberg?' West smiled his fake smile at Jasper.

'Steve and I had a few differences,' Jasper sighed, 'but, you know, I'm just not going to compromise my artistic style.'

'Was it hard to write, star in and direct the movie yourself?'

'Well, it wasn't easy. I had to sit behind the camera, then shout "action", then run in front of the camera really fast and do all the acting stuff. That's never simple. I tripped over twice.'

'And what about you, Rover, could you tell me about the Phat Beats you've been laying down for the soundtrack?' West asked.

'R-Diddly,' Rover said.

'Sorry?'

'He likes to be called R-Diddly, it's his rapper's name,' explained Jasper.

''Sup,' said Rover—sorry, I mean R-Diddly—once again. 'Well, West, we decided that we needed something new for a film as exciting as this. We needed to reinvent music.'

'Wow, that sounds pretty intense. How did you go about it?' West asked, his fixed grin starting to break.

'We took the best bits of folk and jazz, mixed them with some fierce hip-hop beats, and jammed over the top of it.'

'Do either of you play any instruments?'

'Oh yes. My voice is my instrument,' R-Diddly said, nodding.

'For sure,' Jasper agreed earnestly. 'I mean we're pioneers, artists in every sense, so whatever we do is art. Our voices, our minds, also I play a bit of recorder too.'

'Street style!' R-Diddly added.

'I think we've got some footage of you in the studio cutting your new album,' West said, turning to camera.

The action moved to a giant studio with gold discs on the wall. A man with dark glasses nodded as he moved the control panels up and down. Jasper and R-Diddly stood behind a glass booth in front of a microphone. R-Diddly was spitting out some rhymes while Jasper played the recorder with his eyes closed.

'Cats, need to chat, this jam is the story of my homie, J-Spam. The man with the plan on how to get all these cats to chat and rhyme about the time my boy got his jam pumped full of Spam.'

'Two times!' Jasper added before playing a solo on his recorder.

The programme cut back to Jasper and R-Diddly in the studio. 'Did you put all your own money into this project?' West asked.

'Yeah, once Spielberg had left, so did the money, so we self-financed it, along with the album. We hope to make the money back when it becomes a box office smash and also when the album drops.'

'Well, thank you, gentlemen, I'm sure it'll be a huge success. Thank you for talking to Entertainment Xtra.'

'Peas out,' R-Diddly said, making a sign with his paw.

'*Peace* out. It's peace, not peas,' Jasper said under his breath.

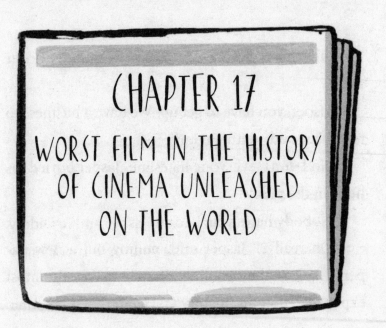

CHAPTER 17
WORST FILM IN THE HISTORY OF CINEMA UNLEASHED ON THE WORLD

'Jasper, Jasper!' Nan cried up the stairs.

'Leave me alone,' came the cry from under the covers.

'Yes,' agreed Rover. 'Leave us alone. We're being impressed.'

'Depressed,' Jasper corrected.

'Depressed, my bad. But we have to get up one day. I don't want to die in this bed with you. It'll be weird. What will the papers say?'

'I don't care what the papers say,' Jasper whimpered. Just then the duvet lifted up and Nan got in too.

'OK, this is getting weirder by the minute,' Rover said.

'Jasper, you have to get up. We have a business to run,' Nan said, getting comfy.

'No I don't, everyone hates me.' Jasper buried his head in the pillow.

'Nobody hates you.'

'Oh really?!' Jasper said, pulling out a newspaper. 'Look at the headline! "Jasper makes the most expensive flop in history!"' He grabbed another.

"'*Jasper: A Spam's Tale* is the worst film in the history of film, and the soundtrack is terrible too!'"

'I think you're overreacting . . .' Nan said calmly. 'It doesn't mean they hate you and think you're an idiot.'

'All right, all right!' Jasper said, grabbing another paper. "'We all hate Jasper and think he's an idiot.'"

'Wow,' Nan said, 'I didn't know *Caravanning Weekly* could be so spiteful.'

'My film was a disaster. People actually booed, seventeen people bought my album, and I'm pretty sure all of those were Rover. I'm a joke!'

'We were number one in Albania for a week,' Rover said. 'That's nothing to be sniffed at.'

'At least the Cat Chat 2000 is going well. You're still the person who made cats talk,' Nan added.

'Yeah, but have you seen this?' Jasper said, grabbing one of the papers again. "'Cats: what are they really thinking?" The article says that more and more cats are being seen huddled together with other cats, looking suspicious.'

'What does that mean?' Nan said.

'I don't know, but they think it's something to do with my invention. So that's why I'm staying under the cover and hiding.'

'I think you might change your mind,' Rover said, looking a bit embarrassed.

'If you're going to tell me that I'm better than this, that I'll bounce back, forget it,' Jasper snapped.

'No, I was going to tell you that I've just dropped one, you know, floated an air biscuit, guffed, trumped, parped my horn, done a botty burp, blown mud, chucked a kaboomer, thrown a methane dart, dropped a fluffy, released a squeaker, blown my bum horn, thrown a tail tickler, released the thunder from down under, done a trouser cough, the toothless one has spoken, felt the gust of a stale wind, cleared the room with a rump roar, played the trouser tuba, started a free jacuzzi with a fowl howl, stepped on a duck. In other words, there's a fire in the hole. You know, a fart,' Rover finally finished. 'Hey, where did everyone go?' He poked his head above the covers.

'We left at "guffed",' Nan said, as she and Jasper left the room. 'But at least you got him out of bed.'

178

Rover and Nan followed Jasper downstairs. The mansion was crawling with newly zapped cats who all stood aside and started to whisper as Jasper went past. But Jasper wasn't paying attention—he was too busy trying to put on his gold slippers. 'Arrgh, these don't fit, someone get me another pair!' he yelled at the nearest passing butler.

'Jasper!' Nan cried, 'don't speak to people like that. You're not too rich to get short, sharp shrift from your old nan, you know!'

'How can you tell me off after all I've done for you? I bought you this house!' Jasper shouted.

'You bought this house for yourself, not me! I didn't ask to move,' Nan shouted back.

'Oh, leave me be,' Jasper said, disappearing towards his lab and slamming the door behind him.

'Leave him, Nan,' Rover said. 'He's just in a bad place. He needs to let off a bit of steam.'

'We could all do with that,' Nan said, grabbing her riding helmet and heading out to the stables. 'It's like I don't know him any more.'

Rover looked around. The place was full of

cats and servants. It didn't feel much like home. He headed towards his electric cat flap and walked out into the garden. In the distance, he could see Nan taking Sunbeam for a spin. Rover took a deep breath and sighed.

'Having fun?' came a familiar voice.

'Arrgh!' Rover jumped. He turned around to see Precious standing behind him. 'ARRGH!' He jumped even higher.

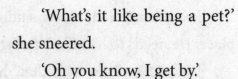

'Still as tough as ever I see,' she tutted.

'Still as bald as an egg I see,' Rover replied sarcastically.

'What's it like being a pet?' she sneered.

'Oh you know, I get by.'

'Don't you ever wish you were in charge? All these humans are slowing us down—we're the cleverest ones on this planet. When will you open your eyes and see what the rest of us can see? Cats should be running the world, not them!'

'Have you been on the catnip?' Rover said, looking utterly bewildered. Precious grabbed him by the throat.

'Listen, it's coming, with or without you. You haven't just made some cats talk, you fool, you've created an army.' Precious pointed through the window into the dining room. Rover struggled free and looked. Suddenly, the house full of cats looked suspicious and scary. Rover turned round.

'What have you done . . .' he trailed off. But it was too late. Precious had gone.

CHAPTER 18
CATS: KNOW THE DANGERS!

Along the alleyways and side streets of Great Britain, there was the smell of revolution in the air— although it could have been cat widdle; it's hard to tell. Like any dark force, it all started with a whisper, an idea, a thought. But soon the whisper began to grow louder and louder. Soon the word spread that the time had come, the time to overthrow humans once and for all. The cats who could talk spread the word among those who couldn't. Without anyone even noticing, an army assembled that stretched up and down the land, ready to obey the every word of Precious.

'Psst!' a smokey grey moggy whispered to a gang sat by the bins. 'Listen, comrades, times are changing. No more will we be human slaves, and under the leadership of Precious we will rise as one. We have a plan in place—you'll know when it is time. Until then, cause as much mayhem as you can. Do you understand? Meow if you do.'

The cats all looked at each other (well, apart from one who was licking his bits). The rest of them meowed.

'Good. Now I have to go and spread the word. Stay strong, comrades—and to you on the floor cleaning yourself, you've missed a bit.'

'Hi, my name's Charlie James. You're listening to a special report. Tonight: the enemy within. Yes, that's right, are we in danger from cats? These cute, fluffy bundles of fun have been human companions for thousands of years, but have they now turned against us? It started out as a few reports of cats behaving strangely after receiving the Cat Chat 2000 procedure, but since then things have become a little more sinister. Cats have been spotted huddled together, whispering. Are they up to something? What are they plotting? We've been speaking to one owner who didn't want to be identified; we'll call her Doris, although her real name is Gertrude. Gertrude—I mean Doris—tell me about your cat, Tiddles.'

'Well, it all started after he got the Cat Chat 2000 treatment. I had some money saved in the bank, you know, a few million, and I decided that as it was only me and Tiddles, I'd have him done. I thought it'd be nice to be able to chat to him at night. So I spent my life savings on having him zapped.'

'I see,' Charlie James said sincerely. 'Then what happened?'

'It started out fine—we'd watch *The Antiques Roadshow* together, have a cuppa and a chat, maybe even a fig roll. Then I noticed Tiddles going out a lot more, chatting to other cats. He seemed to change then, he had more of an attitude. He started complaining about having to use the cat flap, rather than the front door. He wanted his own key. Then I came home one day and found him in my clothes. He was wearing my hat and slippers, watching the TV. He demanded I make him dinner. I wasn't allowed to watch what I wanted any more. Then he started to build a human flap for me. He said that was the only way I could get in and out of the house. He changed the locks. Started giving me my dinner in a bowl. I had to sleep in a basket while he got the master bedroom. He started to bring his cat mates round:

that's when the drinking started. They'd come in from the pub, reeking of beer and pork scratchings. I felt like a prisoner in my own home ... Wait, do you hear a sound? That's him, that's Tiddles. Quick, turn that camera off—everyone out of the human flap!'

Suddenly the footage ended.

It resumed with Charlie James in the studio. 'We had to flee from the house at that point,' he said. 'Doris—or Gertrude, I forget—was in fear for her life. And this pattern of behaviour is being repeated throughout the country. Cats are rising up, their owners are being held hostage by their own pets. There is a mood in the air; it feels like the cats are about to take over the world. The inventor of the Cat Chat 2000 was unavailable for comment. His spokes-person, also known as Nan, said, and I quote, "He's not coming out, he's too busy hiding in his bed like a silly billy. If he doesn't come out soon, I'll have to pull the duvet off him whether he likes it or not." These are indeed desperate times for everyone.'

'SPAM! SPAM! OPEN THIS DOOR IMMEDI-
ATELY!' Mr Dank thumped the door once again.
'SPAAAAAM!'

'All right, keep it down. It's still early,' Nan said,
opening the door and rubbing her eyes. She was
wearing her dressing gown and slippers.

'Where is he? Where's that grandson of yours,
the one that's turned my sweet Precious into a crazy!'

'Now, stop exaggerating and calm down.'

'Calm down?' Mr Dank said, forcing his way in.

'Calm down? She's after me—you should see the way she looks at me. Like I'm dirt. Wait . . . are there any cats in here?' He looked around nervously.

'No,' Nan replied. 'Business has tailed off since all this malarkey has blown up in the news.'

'Phew.'

'Morning, Dank,' Rover said, strolling into the hall.

'ARRGH! I thought you said there were no more cats!' Mr Dank jumped into Nan's arms.

'It's just Rover. He's normal.' Nan was struggling to hold the eighteen stone man in her arms.

'Am I? I mean, I am,' Rover said, not knowing what they were talking about.

'It's all this cat business,' Nan explained.

'Is this about the flowerbeds?' Rover looked worried. 'You said it was fine to do it there.'

'No!' Nan said. 'It's this stuff on the news about cats wanting to take over the world.'

'Oh, yeah, that's not true. I don't want to take over the world. I'm a lover, not a fighter,' Rover said.

'What's all the noise about?' said Jasper, walking in. 'Nan, why are you holding Mr Dank in your arms? Are you two in love? Is he my new grandad?'

'ARRGH!' Mr Dank and Nan yelled. Nan dropped him sharply. 'No, he's here about Precious— apparently she's gone a bit doolally.'

'Doolally? She's gone a bit more than that. Suddenly there are loose tiles on the roof—one nearly hit me on the head the other day. I walked down the stairs this morning, and the banister came off in my hand. I don't feel safe,' Mr Dank whimpered.

'Have you spoken to her about it?' Jasper asked.

'Spoken to her? I don't like being in the same room as her. She has the run of the house now. I sleep in the car! I want my money back, Spam, and I want it back now!'

'What?!' Jasper said.

'Either you fix my cat, or you give me my money back.'

'Fix her?'

'Yes, you made her like this—so fix her. Reverse the process.'

'I can't do that!'

'Why not?' Mr Dank asked.

'Yeah, why not?' Nan added.

'Well, I don't really know how to . . .'

'What? Next you'll be telling me the whole thing was an accident.'

'Err . . . well . . .' Jasper looked at his shoes.

'You have got to be kidding me!' Mr Dank cried, getting his phone out of his pocket.

'Who are you calling?' Rover asked.

'The police. You, young man, are a fraud!'

CHAPTER 19
SPAM BANKRUPT

Thwack came the loud slam of the mallet as the For Sale sign was whacked into the ground. Spam Mansions was in total and utter chaos; everything that had any value was being taken away to pay off the debts. Everyone wanted their money back. All the millions had disappeared as quickly as they'd arrived. Bonzo had taken his hatstand back, gold pants were being snatched off the washing line and taken back to the shop.

The phone had been ringing non-stop for days and Nan was in the kitchen, trying to answer all the calls. All around them men were taking away their belongings: priceless works of art, gold statues, Rover's small but ill-advised collection of platinum medallions from his disco phase. Someone was even taking Sunbeam away, or trying to. She bared her scary teeth and the man backed away.

BIG
DAVE'S
REMOVALS

'I'm sorry, he can't come to the phone,' Nan barked. 'No, he is not able to fix your cat at the moment. Well, I'm sorry to hear that. My advice would be stay away from it and don't turn your back on it. Or get a big dog or something.'

'This is no good,' Rover said, clutching paw-fuls of documents. 'Fifteen new lawsuits have just arrived. As soon as I pay one off, another comes. Good news is that we've sold the football club for à profit.'

'Excellent, how much?' Nan shouted above the noise.

'Seventy-five pence.' Rover grinned. 'Every little helps.'

'Seventy-fiiii . . . oh, never mind. Where's Jasper?'

'Arggh, stop shining the light in my eyes. I'll talk, I'll talk!' Jasper wailed.

'Oops, sorry, I didn't mean to knock the lamp,' the policeman apologized, moving it away from Jasper. 'My name's Chief Inspector Quibble and this is my colleague from the serious fraud office, Stan Figgle. We'd like to have a word with you about all this Cat Chat hullabaloo. It seems you've put a few people's backs up. I won't lie to you, people want you arrested and thrown in jail.'

'WHAT!' Jasper cried. 'JAIL?'

Two men in overalls came in and started carrying away his gold table. 'Oi, do you mind if I finish my cornflakes first?' Jasper said.

'We'll need those too, and your diamond dressing gown,' one of the men said.

'Fine . . .' Jasper huffed. 'Do you want my vest too?'

The men looked at each other.

'I was joking!'

They shuffled off with the table, cornflakes spilling as they went, leaving Jasper in his vest and smalls on a dining room chair, minus the dining bit.

'I don't want to go to jail, please. I'm too young!' Jasper pleaded.

'Don't worry, no one's going to jail. If folk are foolish enough to want a talking cat, then they deserve everything that's coming their way,' Quibble said, shaking his not inconsiderable bonce.

Figgle seemed less accommodating. 'You claim to be a scientist, an inventor. Tell me, how did you invent the Cat Chat 2000? I'm curious.' He smiled a smile that wasn't really a smile.

'Oh yes, the invention, well, you know that ninety-five percent of all inventions are accidents,' Jasper stammered.

'Really?' Figgle snapped.

'Well, I might have made those numbers up slightly, but some inventions really are accidents. Mine was a bit of one . . .'

'How much of it was?'

'Well, all of it.'

The two men sighed. 'Falsely claiming that Cat Chat 2000 is safe, endangering human life, creating a malevolent army of feline killers, operating without a licence. Consider yourself fined.' Figgle slammed down a bill for seventy-five million pounds.

Jasper sighed and got his cheque book out. Once the police had left, he sat alone on his chair. By now the place had pretty much been stripped down to the bare bones. He'd lost everything. The worst news of all was that they'd have to move back into their old house. Where was Sunbeam going to live? His nan would have to go back to work. He'd been so stupid. He was no inventor, he was a boy. What had he thought he was doing? He went upstairs and grabbed his normal clothes. It felt strange, like he was slipping back into his old skin.

'There you are,' Nan said, smiling. She was packing up her stuff, getting ready for the move home. Jasper couldn't look her in the eye.

'Sorry, Nan, sorry that we have to go back. I've really messed things up. You must be disappointed.'

'No. I won't have that, I won't have you feeling sorry for yourself. OK, the money came and went, but we had a great adventure. It was fun while it lasted. Sometimes things don't work out, but we've been here before. We always survive.' Nan gave him a cuddle.

'Yeah, you're right.' Jasper sighed. 'At least the phone's stopped ringing.'

'Actually, the phone's been taken away.'

'That's even better news!' Jasper laughed. He looked round and saw that the debt collectors had left a TV behind. He switched it on. There was his face on every channel. Telling the story of how he'd gone from being the world's richest boy to a total laughing stock.

'We interrupt this regular news programme to give you this special report. According to the MOD, the number of cat attacks on humans has increased significantly in the last few hours. Governments fear a major offensive is in progress.'

Jasper and Nan looked at each other.

'Oh no, this is awful. I can't believe I may have accidentally killed the human race.' Jasper could hardly watch as the TV showed humans stuck up trees, while cats circled below.

'Unless something is done, and done soon, we could all be in real danger. We urge people to stay indoors and away from cats or places where cats might be. The backs of sofas, on top of the radiator, near TVs that are showing the snooker. Use common sense, people!' the news reporter yelled. 'Wait, did anyone hear a meow . . . ? They're in the studio!' The picture tilted wildly to one side before the screen went blank.

'Where have you been?' Rover said, rushing upstairs. 'It's all kicking off out there, we need to go. He's waiting for us!'

'Who?' said Jasper.

'The Prime Minister, of course!'

CHAPTER 20
PRIME MINISTER ISSUES STATE OF EMERGENCY

Jasper, Nan and Rover ran outside. There was a motorcade on the drive—police bikes and patrol cars flanking a black car that sat in the middle of the convoy. What looked like a small boy in sunglasses opened the car door for them.

'Thank you,' said Jasper. 'What's going on, who are you?'

'The name's Twigg, Kevin Twigg—licence to get all up in your face!' the lad said, lifting up his glasses.

'What?' Nan said, twiddling her hearing aid.

'Only joking. It's just something I like to say to people.' The boy slammed the door.

'Blimey, is it me or are the secret service getting younger and younger?' Nan said in disbelief.

The car sped through the suburbs, and as they drove, Jasper could see tanks being sent the other way. There were helicopters overhead, darting in the air like giant mechanical mosquitos. Jasper winced as he watched families being chased from their homes by hissing cats.

A phone inside the car door started to ring. Rover looked at Nan, Nan looked at Jasper. Slowly, Jasper lifted up the receiver.

'Hello . . .' he said tentatively.

'Hello!' came a cheery voice. 'Is that Jasper Spam?'

'Yes.'

'Aha, excellent, my name's Joe Perkins. I am the PM, that's Prime Minister to you. How goes it?'

Jasper gasped. He put his hand over the receiver and whispered to the others, 'It's the Prime Minister!' He went back to the phone. 'Hello, sir. I'm well. How are you?' Jasper didn't know whether you were supposed to ask prime ministers that, but he wanted to be as polite as he possibly could given the circumstances.

'I'm good, well, apart from this whole "cats are going to kill us all and take over the world" palaver, you know.'

'Yeah, I know,' Jasper replied, trying to sound apologetic. 'I'm sorry about that.'

'Ah, don't worry, these things happen. I nearly

blew up China the other day, when I accidentally pressed the wrong button at work. The blue one is for the coffee machine, the red one is for all the big bombs . . . oh wait, I don't think I was supposed to tell you that. Anyhoo, I was wondering if I could get your help—well, not just me, the rest of the world too. I was wondering if you could make all the cats be normal again,' the PM said in a chummy way.

'I would, sir, but I don't know how. The whole thing was an accident. I don't know how it happened and I don't know how to reverse it.' Jasper sighed.

'Listen, I know a thing or two about accidents. Life can take you by surprise. All I know is that you have to take advantage of these things when they happen. I believe in you. I think if anyone can fix it, you can, Jasper.'

Jasper listened quietly—he didn't know what to say. They were right, all of them. Nan, the Prime Minister. Now was not the time to feel sorry for himself, now was the time to fix things. He didn't know how, but he knew he had to give it a try.

'OK, Prime Minister. I'll do my best. I need a bit

of time, but I'll try and figure out this whole thing.'

'Brilliant work!' Joe Perkins yelled with delight. 'Right, I have to go. Ajay has lost Gibraltar to the Spanish in a game of Rock, Paper, Scissors . . . Ajay, I told you that's not how these things work!' With that, the line went dead.

'Well?' Nan said, looking nervous.

'I'm going to fix this.' Jasper smiled.

'That's my boy!' said Nan.

'Boom!' Rover grinned, as they pulled into their old drive.

Nan unlocked the front door and dashed in to put the kettle on, the way nans do after any time out of the house.

'Before we go in, I want you to have this.' Rover said pushing an envelope into Jasper's hand. It was my last few quid, I went to the shop and . . .'

'Tell me later,' Jasper said putting it down.

'We need to figure this out. There's something I don't understand. If all the cats are going bad, why haven't I?' Rover scratched one of his ears.

'Yeah, I can't figure that out either,' Jasper said.

Nan came in with the tea and some Jammy Dodgers. 'Well, I'm no expert,' she said, plonking the tray down on the coffee table, 'but could it be to do with the fact that the laser was fired into a mirror. It might have doubled the intensity of the zap and genetically altered the chemical balance inside the cats' heads, making them all evil.' She dunked her biscuit.

Jasper and Rover looked at each other, then at Nan.

'What?' she asked. 'You pick a few things up, zapping cats all day. We can't all spend our time gallivanting around in Hollywood making terrible folk-infused hip hop and buying football clubs.'

'Fair point,' Jasper said.

'No wait, she's right! I think she's on to something!' Rover gasped.

'The mirror must have changed the positive charge to a negative charge,' Jasper said, figuring it out. 'That means if we reverse the charge, and blast the cats with a positive charge, it should cancel out the effect. Then they'd be back to normal. Just ordinary cats.' Jasper grinned. 'I've done it, I've finally done something right. We've figured it out Nan! All we need now is a guinea pig.'

'Or even better, a cat!' Rover said helpfully.

'Yesss,' Jasper said patiently. 'I need to check it works—I can't get it wrong this time. What if it makes things worse?'

Just at that second there was the most awful sound imaginable, a screech that made your teeth curl. Everyone turned round. There was Precious, her claws slowly scratching the window. Her eyes were filled with hate and her grin was as wide as can be.

'Can't you just ring the doorbell like everyone else, you nut job?' Rover snapped.

'I'm not like everyone else,' Precious hissed through the window.

'This may be a long shot, but are you angry because you're bald as an egg? I'd be really cross if I looked like that too. I mean, you're probably just cold. I still have some of my funky chunky cardigans left from my fashion line if you want one. It might cheer you up and you might be less likely to take over the world,' Rover suggested hopefully.

Precious hopped down from the window and within seconds had burst through the cat flap.

'Do you know what I hate about you, Rover?' she snarled.

'Is it my dashing good looks and oh-so-blue eyes?'

'No.'

'Is it my ability to moonwalk?'

'NO!'

'OK, OK, long shot . . . is it my acting skills? I did get an honourable mention in *Vets Monthly* for my recent performance.'

'If you don't shut up, I'm going to eat you for dinner,' Precious barked. Well, I say barked, I mean she replied in a gruff manner. She didn't bark like a dog, although I wouldn't put anything past her. 'It's the fact that you love pretending to be human so much. It's truly pathetic.'

'Pathetic!' Rover yelled. 'I'll tell you what's pathetic—trying to divide us. Cats have got along perfectly well with humans for thousands of years, then you come along and suddenly it's all-out war. You might not want to hear this, but we cats need humans and they need us. I've been looking after

Nan for years just as much as she's been looking after me. It's chaos out there, and it's all thanks to you. And for what? Nothing. You are the pathetic one—you're full of hate. You're miserable and lonely, you push everyone away because you don't know how to love and have friends.'

'Why you little . . . !' Precious screamed, jumping straight at Rover.

'Run, boy, run!' Nan cried.

CHAPTER 21
PRIME MINISTER ISSUES STATE OF EMERGENCY

Rover hurtled out of the back door. Down the path both of them hurtled, like something out of a cartoon, fur flying everywhere. Rover scampered into the shed, looked around nervously for somewhere to hide. But it was too late. Precious burst in, coming to a stuttering halt. She smiled, and began to laugh in that way all evil people tend to laugh.

'Looks like you've run out of places to hide,' she cackled.

Jasper and Nan crashed in a few seconds later.

'Leave him alone!' Nan cried.

Rover jumped up onto the window ledge. Was this it, was he about to be cat on toast? He looked at Nan, he looked at Jasper.

'NOW!' he yelled.

Jasper put the envelope down and hit the switch on the wall. Then he grabbed the mallet and flung it backwards.

'Nooooo . . . !' Precious screamed. It was a trap, she'd been cornered. She leapt towards the window but it was too late.

There was a crash and a flash as the laser fired, but this time Jasper grabbed the mirror and held it in place. There was a familiar howl and the distinct smell of singed fur in the air, followed by a puff of smoke.

'Oh my!' Nan cried in horror and she ran over to the window ledge. 'Rover, speak to us.' But he was out cold.

'Oh no! Rover, please say something,' Jasper said, holding his cat's limp paw. Precious began to open her eyes. She looked around and meowed. She seemed different, less evil, back to her normal weird-looking self. She could no longer talk, and she no longer seemed interested in trying to overthrow humanity. All she wanted to do was stretch and do that thing cats do when they rub themselves up around someone's legs. Then slowly but surely, Rover opened his eyes. He looked around and opened his mouth.

'Meow,' he said contently.

'You're OK!' Jasper said, hugging Rover and then his Nan. 'Can you speak?'

Rover meowed once again.

'Oh, he's probably just joking, like he did before,' said Nan. But Rover wasn't joking. He really was just a normal cat again, the most extraordinary normal cat there's ever been. One that sacrificed everything to save the world—to save Jasper.

'That was the only way we were going to put an end to this. We had to fix Precious, and he knew the only way to do it was to lay a trap.' Jasper sighed, realizing finally what Rover had done. 'They've both been turned back to normal cats again. Rover knew how to provoke her until she was angry enough to chase him down here. What a brilliant cat.'

Jasper and Nan returned to the living room. 'I need to phone the Prime Minister,' Jasper said, 'tell him we know how to turn all the cats back to normal again.'

At that second, the doorbell rang, and there stood a horse chewing on what looked like a lampost. Not just any horse, but Sunbeam.

'Oh look, she must have followed us home.' Nan squeezed her delightedly. 'Room for another pet?' she cried.

'Yeah, why not,' Jasper said with a smile.

A while later, Nan was in the middle of fixing tea, beans on toast for two, hay for Sunbeam and garlic-roasted poussin in a shallot and red wine *jus* for Rover. Well he'd had quite a traumatic day, so Nan decided to spoil him.

'Yes, that's right, PM. Just tell your military people to fire the lasers into the mirror and tickety-boo, all the cats should be back to normal in no time,' Jasper was saying.

'Well done, Jasper!' the PM said. 'You should come to Downing Street some time. We've just opened up a new water slide in the Chancellor's office. He's furious about it, but I think it's a hoot!'

'That would be great, thank you!' Jasper grinned. 'Can I bring my nan?'

'Of course,' the PM replied. 'So Jasper, what are you going to do once all this has blown over?'

'Funny you should mention that . . .' Jasper said, turning to Nan and Sunbeam.

CHAPTER 22
HORSE SPOTTED ON THE M5

'You join us here on a lovely spring day for the annual Grand National. At the front, with just a few fences to go, is Sunbeam, ridden by Marjory Lilly Spam, who looks like she's going to be the oldest winner of the race at . . . well, no one's really sure of her age, but we've narrowed it down to between seventy and eighty-four. Today she's riding Sunbeam, the biggest and, fair to say, the most ferocious horse I've ever seen. At one point, she actually jumped over another horse. I've never seen that before. And here she comes up to the last but one fence and it's

Sunbeam on the outside, she's just a few feet ahead of Goes Like Stink who's in second place. Goes Like Stink looks like she's gaining on Sunbeam, yes, they're getting closer all the time. Mrs Spam, or Nan as she's known to the world, is really giving it the beans now, she's out of the saddle and shouting something at Sunbeam.'

'IF YOU LOSE THIS, I'LL GIVE YOU A THICK EAR!' Nan yelled into Sunbeam's ear.

'Probably words of encouragement,' the commentator added. 'And we're into the final furlong, only a few more yards to go, Goes Like Stink is closing in fast. Well, I've never seen that before. Sunbeam has just turned round and roared at Goes Like Stink . . . yes . . . Goes Like Stink has stopped racing and done a big wee. Sunbeam and Nan are going to cross the line. They're going to win the Grand National!'

Everyone was cheering. Well you would, at the sight of a little old lady winning the most dangerous horse race in the world. Back by the finishing line, Jasper, decked out in top hat and tails that he'd made out of cardboard and an old curtain, was leaping about cheering. Next to him was Rover, also in top hat and tails, meowing loudly. Even though Rover was to all intents and purposes a normal cat again, he still liked to be by Jasper's side.

It had been a few weeks since the world had nearly been taken over by cats, since Jasper had brought the world to the brink of annihilation before saving it again. The world had pretty much moved on and forgiven Jasper. The Spams were still broke,

Nan had taken up her cleaning job for Mr Dank again. They needed the money and he treated her much better now; partly because he'd learnt a valuable life lesson about how to treat your fellow humans, and partly because he was scared to be left alone in the house with Precious for too long. Even after the reversal treatment, she had remained a vile mog, but she'd cheered up considerably since Mr Dank had bought her a cardigan. Jasper was about to start at a new school. It had an excellent science department, with science clubs after school, so there was no need to break in and set off the fire alarms in the name of invention.

Jasper high-fived Rover, who held out a celebratory paw. 'We did it! We won! I can't believe it, Rover.'

Nan came into the winners' enclosure still riding Sunbeam, who continued to roar and snarl at anyone who went near her. Nan reached into her pocket and pulled out a raw steak. Most horses prefer sugar lumps, but raw meat seemed to do it for Sunbeam. It's what made her a cold-blooded racing machine.

'Good gal,' Nan said, tickling her ear. 'We totally

crushed them; that's why Nanna loves you to bits,' she continued in her cutest baby voice. 'You're a monster, aren't you?'

'Well done, Nan!' Jasper cried. 'I knew you could do it!'

'Thanks lad. I'm thinking about entering her for the Kentucky Derby next month. Plus the winnings will come in handy!' She waved her winner's cheque with a grin. 'We should have enough to pay for the gas and electricity now.'

Nan seemed so happy, but suddenly Jasper felt sad. He'd had more money than he knew what to do with and he'd lost the lot. Had he got too greedy? Maybe—if he'd been more thorough he wouldn't have been sued by everyone. All he knew was that they were back to exactly where they'd started a few months ago. Rover rubbed his head against Jasper's knees, sensing that he was sad. He looked up and gave him a comforting meow.

'Good ol' Rover, you can always cheer me up.'

It was dark by the time they got home. It had taken a while for them to ride back on Sunbeam and the motorway had been pretty busy. Admittedly, the sight of two people and a cat doing seventy in the fast lane on a horse had caused the odd traffic jam, but they didn't have a car, so what can you do? Nan climbed off, and led Sunbeam to the garden to eat nettles and drink some septic water from the pond. It was her favourite.

'I'll put some beans on in a mo,' Nan said.

'Lovely,' Jasper said, picking the flies out of his teeth.

'It's our last tin. We need some more shopping.' Nan looked in the biscuit tin for some coins. 'If only our ship would come in!'

As Nan looked at the last few pence in her hand, Rover started meowing wildly and circling around their feet.

'What is it, lad? I'll get you some dinner too,' Nan said. Rover started clawing the back door.

'I think he wants to go out.' Jasper opened the door.

But all Rover did was meow loudly.

'I think he wants us to follow him . . .'

Jasper and Nan followed Rover down towards the shed. The cat started clawing at the door to get in. Jasper pushed it open. He hadn't been in there for weeks, it felt odd to be back.

'Rover, I'm not going to zap you again. I can't risk it. What if I get it wrong and hurt you?' Jasper said.

'I don't think that's what he wants,' Nan said. She hit the button to turn on the lights, and various machines started to whizz and spring into life. Rover jumped onto the window shelf and picked something up in his mouth.

'What's that?' Nan said.

'It's a letter. Rover gave it to me the night we got back. I must have put it down when he and Precious had that fight. I'd forgotten all about it,' Jasper said, taking the envelope from Rover's mouth. 'Listen, Rover, you don't have to fetch the post for us, you're not a dog.'

Rover interrupted with a meow.

'OK, OK, I'll open it.' Nan opened it slowly. Her confused expression turned into a smile that started off very slowly before turning into a full-scale beam. 'Hahahahaa! It's a betting slip. Rover must have done it ages ago! It's for me and Sunbeam to win the Grand National at five thousand to one!' she laughed.

'What does that mean?!' Jasper said.

'It means Rover thought I was going to win the Grand National, and we're rich!' Nan cried.

'What?!' Jasper leapt in the air. 'Oh lad, you've done it! And I'll tell you one thing right now, we're not moving or buying any more of those gold pants.'

All three of them grouped together for a big hug and started jumping around uncontrollably.

Nan kicked her legs in the air, Jasper did some excellent robotic dancing and Rover moonwalked along the shelf, before tripping and falling off it. He tried to grab onto the side, but all he managed to grasp was the mallet. He held on tight to it, spinning as he fell, the mallet head flying off towards the test tubes that began to fall like dominoes towards the laser machine.

Suddenly there was a flash as the laser beam fired a zap around the shed. It pinged off the mirror, the can of oil and the lawnmower blades. There was a loud flash and a crack. Jasper hit the ground at once, as did Rover. The two of them looked at each other, then back at Nan. Her eyes were crossed and a single thread of black smoke was coming off her bottom.

Jasper gulped.

Rover gulped.

'Nan, are you OK? Nan . . .?' Jasper pleaded. 'Say something.'

'Meow!' Nan cried.

'Meow!' Rover grinned.

'I can speak cat!'